Shimmering MEADOW RANCH

The Sawyer Family

ROBIN MILLER

NEWMAN SPRINGS PUBLISHING
320 Broad Street
Red Bank, NJ 07701

First originally published by Newman
Springs Publishing 2023

ISBN 978-1-63881-995-0 (Paperback)
ISBN 978-1-63881-996-7 (Digital)

Printed in the United States of America

CONTENTS

Back from the Drive

It was a beautiful summer morning. The sun glistened off the dew on the webs that were spun between the leaved branches that line the mountain's dirt path.

The light breeze with a hint of forest scent filled the air. I lie, looking up at the blue sky for a moment. I take a deep breath of fresh air, check the time, and I jump to my feet. With my left hand, I grab the withers, kick my right leg over—I'm on! Dapple has been my horse since I was five years old. He is white with black spots on his rump and speckles on his face. We are one when we ride, and he has a calm disposition about him. His personality is like no other horses we have. He is pretty old, so I go easy on him, although he still loves to run. I let him pick his time to let loose.

I hear my mother ringing the dinner bell. I did not realize it was that late. I must have fallen asleep, and my brothers are closer than I thought with the

1

herd. I walk my dapple-gray Appaloosa stallion down the path swiftly and out onto the field.

Dapple was running full force until I saw my mother on the veranda, waiting for everyone. I slow to a trot as not to stir up dust. I notice she has the laundry hanging on the line strung from the barn to the porch on the second story of our farmhouse. I slide off Dapple, run to the veranda, give her a peck on the cheek. I apologize for being late.

I sit on the bench at the long picnic table under the large oak tree that shades most of that side of our yard. I love this old tree; it holds a lot of memories for us as children. My siblings and I spent a lot of time under this tree growing up. Our tire swing used to hang from this low-lying branch for many years. Joe, Jacob, Joshua, Rachel, and Jeremiah were married under this tree, and picnics in the summers are endless. Our tree is as old as the land the ranch is on. This is the story our father tells everyone when we hold a family gathering under our large shade tree. Due to how tall and round this tree is, the rings inside the tree must be at least three hundred, if not more.

As I look across the center of the table, I see fried chicken, potatoes, gravy, freshly made honey-buttered rolls, salad, and two pitchers, one full of lemonade and the other of sun-made iced tea.

I see my brothers coming in across the field, with our border collies—Snow, Sky, Storm, and Rain—my father trailing behind. The dust from the summer drought is swirling up around them with the smell of oncoming rain in the air. They tie their horses at the post and wash up at the pump from the spring at the front of our house.

I hear them talking about the cattle drive, mentioning the coyote that almost got an Angus calf. As they came through the meadow with the herd, a mountain lion tried to stalk one of the two pregnant heifers, which Jacob saved as Joshua got the hunter's attention. What an exciting drive!

My father can hardly wait until the end of the month so they can get the cattle that are in the barn to market. I have learned so much over the years growing up on our ranch. I have learned that a calf must be three to five months old before they are branded with our ranch logo. Moving the cattle, which is called herding, is crucial to the soil and property of the ranch. My brothers taught me how to "cut ride" to handle cattle while on a cattle drive. Cut riding is being quicker than the cattle to keep the strays from wondering away from the rest of the herd. Then there were times I had to help cut a few cattle from the herd.

3

I am never invited to ride on a drive to move the cattle from one grazing area to another. I do, however, get asked to ride out to check on them every now and again but never to do any vigorous riding or rounding them up to move. Father boasts, "It's men's work." My father has other ranch hands that come and help while my brothers are away at college.

The ranch hands who help us are friends of my parents. Jim, who owns the feed mill, loves to get away for a few days on a drive. There are several men from two towns over, who are friends of my father and love to help as well.

Our ranch is one hundred thousand acres with five hundred plus head of cattle. My brother Joe gets the word out to the cowboys who helped herd cattle last year. These text messages usually bring extra cowboys, as the cowboys who are notified tell their friends. Jim and my father run the young cowboys through cut riding and strength. They practice how to rope steers; they are shown how to use the collies to help as well. Jim and our father brand, vaccinate, and release the young calves. The young cowboys pick up how to rope, cut, and herd pretty quickly. Jim stated, "It's exciting to watch the young up and coming cowboys do their stuff." They remarked it reminds them of the good old days.

Hitchin' Up

My father, Joe, is a rugged, refined tall dark-haired, brown-eyed cowboy. He has done ranch work for many ranchers growing up as a young boy into his teenage years. He knows a lot about ranch life.

His parents, Lydia and Jeremiah, who passed on before I was born, rented (never owned) a home and always worked for others, although they didn't have to, they appeared to be scraping to get by. They were well-to-do but "tight in the purse strings," as my father puts it. In other words, they knew how to save money.

My grandparents were happy and so much in love. They were cut from strong cloth. Their life depended on their determination and skill. They had to live and get by even though they struggled at times. This showed their child, my father Joseph, to be a good husband, hard worker, have a life plan, and faith first of all. My father had a plan of doing more for his family when he had one. He met my mother, and their life took flight. Everything was falling into place.

My mother's name is Abigail. She is tall, slender, with long dark hair, and the kindest soul you could ever meet. Her parents, Bertha and Ralph, had a little money. They owned a small but well-known business that when her parents passed on, Mother inherited. She ran it for a while then sold it for a nice chunk of change.

She was the oldest of three children. When she was eight, her siblings, at the young age of six, passed on from a horrible disease. Mother has told us a little but never spoke in depth about her siblings. My siblings and I don't know if she had sisters, brothers, or possibly one of each. We don't ask. We do know it is on her mind; at times she starts talking about them, and we listen to try to learn and know them, only to have our mother shut down, so we really have no idea what went on, although we do know they were too young to leave her so early. We only know our mother loves and misses them. It is a mystery to us as to what happened, but one day, we hope she opens up to tell us.

Both our parents brought the money they had to their marriage, enough to purchase one hundred thousand acres to start their dream, Shimmering Meadow Ranch. With the money that remained, they purchased other necessities: four stock horses, an Aberdeen Angus bull, and a few Simmental and Charolais cattle. This is how it all began.

Thoughts of Yesterday

I recall Mother's talking of the early days of ranch life with Father. They would wake up super-early in the morning, saddling up their horses and loading two others with supplies for a possible overnight stay with the cattle. They would set up camp, brand the new calves with the ranch logo, make sure all the cattle were together in the same area, and settle in for the night. She would help round up and move the cattle from one grazing area to another when needed, then bring them back to the barn for a couple days.

Father would have his friend Jim and a few others from the neighboring towns go out to stay in the grazing fields when needed for a week or so, just so the cattle could eat off the land. Mother and Father would then ride out to check on the cattle and the hired ranch hands to see if they needed anything.

When bad weather was coming or when seasons changed, they would bring the cattle closer to the barn. By the time winter came, the cattle would be housed in the barn for a few months to fatten them up for market. The cattle would be picked up by large cattle rigs and hauled off for...well, you know.

This became my parents' ritual for the first two years until my mother was pregnant with Joseph.

My parents had a well-known, respectable ranch within four years after they were hitched. Things were falling into place. It all changed when my brothers were old enough to travel by horseback with our father to ride and help. He purchased the border collies after a year or two of working with my brothers and the cattle on the ranch. The herd was getting larger now, and they needed the extra help. The border collies—Snow, Sky, Storm, and Rain—are a big help with herding the cattle, and they make the perfect ranch hands to help my father and brothers!

They are beautiful, smart, and well-behaved. Snow is white as the first fallen snow. Sky is a pretty gray; she looks like a blue sky on a clear day. Storm is a combination of multicolored golden, gray, white with black, and somewhat tortoise shell. Rain is blue-gray with white speckles. To hear my brothers yell to the collies during the cattle drive, you would think they were broadcasting the weather.

VALUES AND RESPONSIBILITIES

Our childhood was filled with chores, which gave us responsibilities. These things shaped us as teenagers and young adults, as well as made us who we are today—responsible adults with values, ambition to work and help others.

I often wonder how we were able to get the chores done after we started attending public school. After getting home from school every night, we would eat and go right to the chores. Chores at night were a little more involved than the chores in the morning before school. We definitely needed a shower after night chores. If we had time, we could watch television but only after the homework was completed.

My and Rachael's morning chores were tending to the smaller critters on the farm. These are my chores now that Rachel has moved on with her life to the big city. We collected eggs and fed the chickens, horses, kitties, and border collies when they weren't off to the cattle-grazing area for the day.

Barn to a Home

Years ago, before all us kids came along, our house was a large barn my parents, with the help of a few friends, made into a house. Took some work, my father adds when he tells that story. The barn had a roof that was fallen in on one side, with barn boards missing every so often on the other. There were high weeds/brush, stickers of many kinds surrounding the old barn as if to swallow it. Father also adds it was a diamond in the rough.

The barn since then took formation of the Sawyer family dream. The house has four bedrooms, four full bathrooms, with a powder room off the kitchen, not to mention the walk-in cooler Father kept and built the kitchen around it. The walk-in cooler was a great idea to incorporate into the house. It comes in handy when family is home for the holidays.

For some reason the walls on that corner of the house were made of large stones, which are cool in temperature in the summer and downright cold in the winter. He also added a beautiful wood to the door on the kitchen side to not have it look like a cooler door. Mother loves how he fit this into our kitchen; the finishing touch on the door is beautiful. Everyone thinks it is an extra pantry or a way to the basement.

The living room is the entire back half of the bottom of the barn with a large two-sided stone fireplace, which is in the center between the living room and dining room/kitchen area. Hardwood floors run throughout the entire home.

The living room has two nice full comfortable recliners, an extralarge wraparound sofa with large pillows and a few throw blankets placed on the backs of the sofa, a large ottoman to match with a red maple coffee table in the center. The living room has three large windmill ceiling fans across the top of the barn board ceiling to circulate the warm air in the winter and the cool air in the summer.

The kitchen and dining room are on the front side of the bottom of the house. The kitchen has a lot of counter space with a kitchen bar off the island where my family gathers to drink coffee and where we have short discussions. One would say this island is our meeting place.

The entire downstairs of our home smells like apple cinnamon all year round because of Mother's baking the signature pie for the Grilling Post. The Grilling Post is a restaurant owned by a close family friend of my parents and also in-laws of my brother Jacob.

The dining room has a long farm table made of hickory with two captain's chairs at opposite ends and twelve chairs in between. Father and the boys made this table and chairs many years ago. This dining room is very active on Sundays, Easter, Thanksgiving, and Christmas, not to mention all the special occasions in between.

Since we would be spending most of our family time in these rooms as we grew up, these rooms on the first floor are huge. Joseph always had his own room. Joseph's room is a master suite on the first floor on the opposite side of the living room from our parents' room. Father, with the help of Joe when he was a young boy, built the barnwood full sized bed. There is a beautiful blanket that is draped over the bottom of the bed that Mother put together using pieces of Joe's flannel button-down shirts when he was a boy of five years old. This quilt holds a lot of memories. To my brother Joseph, it is a piece of our mother's love, a family heirloom Joseph will always cherish. Our father and mother's bedroom mirrors my brother Joe's room.

Jeremiah, Joshua, and Jacob always shared the entire attic, which is as long and wide as the house. The attic has a full bathroom as well. There are three full-size log beds also graced with quilts my mother made from the jean material since the triplets were five years of age. The boys treasure these quilts as well. They brag the stitches are mother's love that holds their quilt together.

The beds are opposite. The front wall of the attic has two beds near the far corners, with one along the center on the wall toward the back of the house. They have matching bedside tables, a cedar bench-chest at the bottom of each bed, a chest of drawers, a large walk-in closet, and a medium-sized full-length mirror hanging on the wall outside the closet to the right framed in wood to match their beds. Mother had Father hang that mirror soon after the boys were nine years old. The triplets thought they were going to dress for church in a way Mother did not approve. She sent them back upstairs to dress in a proper suit for church.

The attic is what we call the penthouse suite. The attic ceiling was done with stained cedar, four large windmill ceiling fans for air circulation, and three windows in each side of the barn roof with large windowsills. There are two windows on either end as well.

Rachel and I shared a room just as big on the second floor. We each had our own side of the large room. We also had a full bathroom in the center of the front wall across from the stairs. Our study area was located at our large windows on opposite sides of the room with our beds placed on the far sides of the room against the far corners. Rachel and I were talkers. Our parents agree the house would get sleep with us on opposite ends of everything.

Our beds were full-size barnwood made by our father and brothers. We also had matching bedside tables on either side of our beds with lamps. The dressers, which matched our beds, were on the wall across from our beds. Rachel and I had two walk-in closets on either side of our bathroom. Our ceiling was made of barnwood and had large windmill ceiling fans.

Our beds were graced with quilts Mother made from our dress material since when we were five years old, using our hair ribbon as the ties. Rachel's and my blanket were mended by Mother more times than we care to remember. The sun rose on my side of the room, and set on Rachael's side of the room.

Beautiful views! The rooms are all empty now, but a few days before the holidays, these rooms and this house jump with excitement!

My parents' home is in the center of the acreage, which sits on the lushest green area of grass we have ever seen. Father explained years ago the cattle grazed closer to the barn, which has given us an unbelievably lush green lawn since the barn is now our home. The old farmhouse is beautiful!

IT'S ALL RELATIVE

Joe was the firstborn and the eldest. Then four years later came identical triplets Joshua, Jacob, and Jeremiah. My parents were blessed with four boys. After four years, my parents wanted a girl. That's when Rachel and I came along. Yes, you guessed it! I am one of identical twins. The chances of having multiple identical births were high for our parents. Our parents call it a blessing from God. We call it amazing! How did they keep everyone straight?

That old house was soon filled with the pitter-patter of little feet, ranging from twelve to newborn. There were six kids, and the house was so busy, so full of life!

When we get together with my brothers, their wives, my sister, and her husband, we hear how easy it was to have all six of us to clean the large farmhouse, do the ranch work, and cook meals. Our mother deserves bragging rights. As time goes on, our family grows even larger.

We are part of a somewhat religious family, as you may have already guessed. My brothers look exactly like my father—tall, dark, and handsome with that rugged cowboy look but younger. My sister and I look like our mother. Rachel and I have long dark-brown hair, and large brown eyes. I'm always in my bib overalls, cut-off shorts and jeans. Rachel is in dresses or dress clothes, which is how you can tell us apart these days.

Cowboys in
Training

I was five years old, and this was probably the first age I remember something from my life as a child. Since our brother Joe was the oldest, he already had his stock horse buckskin named Bo that he broke to ride with the help of Father. Joe told us that Father knew what he was doing when it came to breaking a horse. Joe and Bo were the best of friends.

The triplets got their horses when they were colts. These colts were stock buckskin like Joe's. Their names were Blitz, Blaze, and Breeze. These colts had to be tamed and trained. The colts and the boys grew together. Joe told us it was a sight to watch.

Bo, Blitz, Blaze, and Breeze passed of old age a few years ago. My brothers have Morgan horses now. Joe's horse is named Walker, Jeremiah's horse is named Kentucky, Joshua's horse is named Diesel, and Jacob's horse is named Remington, or Remi for short.

Rachel and I each had dapple-gray Appaloosa stallions. As they got older, the gray spots turned black. What a wild package they were, Dapple and Stally. We had fall time, throw-off time, and times we just wanted to give up and call it a day. Between our father and brother Joe, they kept working with us.

It finally happened. We broke our colts. Over time, we became one with our horses. We trusted them; they trusted us. My sister's horse actually lay so she could get on him. You know horses grow so fast. Rachel and I were tiny. Dapple learned how to get me on his back as well. He would put his head down, and I would climb on him behind his ears, and he would lift me up. I would then flip around when I reached his back. Horses are amazingly intelligent.

Maybe I have this memory because all the bumps and bruises made such an impression on me.

EDUCATION

We believe they invested their money, and it drew a lot of interest over the years. Our parents paid the total college bill for each of us. I guess our parents wanted what was best for us and to not start our future with major college loans. Let me just add not all of us went to a college that was too expensive. I just wanted to do something that I was not going to spend another lifetime at education before I started living life.

On the other hand, my siblings looked at college as a means to not work as hard as father does on the ranch, which I guess is a good life lesson. We all knew we had to work hard to get anywhere in life; no one would get a free ride, so to speak. Our parents told us you need to pull your weight and do something good for yourself, your family, and the people around you.

My brothers ideal mapped-out plans are college, wife, a career, and children. I cannot wait to be an aunt! My parents know when the boys move on, it will happen pretty quickly. Joshua is going to have his doctorate in architecture; he was a doodler. Joshua designed the barn using his architectural skills. My parents say they are fortunate to have the barn as this was the first project Joshua took on at the end of his education and start of his career. He is twenty-seven years old and hanging his shingle in a few days. My parents are proud of Joshua.

The barn is a gigantic U shape. Our horses are in the right top of the barn; the cattle are herded in on the entire lower part of the barn; and our tack, furrier supplies, and food for the animals are in the center top of the barn. The work area and the tractors are in the top left side of the barn.

The barn is a nice, safe, warm place with electric and water, not to mention a full bathroom with many other amenities. The attic of the barn is where our bunkhouse is for the ranch hands. Many live here all year round as this is their full-time job.

Jeremiah has been studying a lifetime to be a cardiologist. He completed twelve years of education now and only has five years left of residency. He is awaiting his interview from six cardiology specialty facilities. He will do a fellowship for a year at a facility of his choice if accepted. We are not sure if he will open his own practice or work for a group of cardiologists in a larger practice. I am sure we will find out before he finishes his fellowship. Jeremiah is twenty-seven and will be thirty-three years old when he becomes a cardiac surgeon/specialist.

Jacob, on the other hand, is a nuclear physicist. The knowledge Jacob has of atom structures and their properties, he knows what makes the atom react. He also talks about gravity. Jacob's brain is loaded with all kinds of scientific information. Jacob has his MS. He is ending his second year of completing his PhD. He has one and a half years to complete his lab then will finish. He will be twenty-nine when he is ready to start his career. My parents are proud, excited, and could not be happier for all their boys!

My brothers were on the Internet, completing college courses as they could while in their sophomore year of high school. Other curricula my siblings completed at a local accredited college in the evenings while they attended their last three years of high school.

We were homeschooled until eighth grade. Mother gave us homework like there was no tomorrow; it's possible that giving us so much schoolwork pushed us to want more education. Our mother always assured us, "Anything you need to know you can learn right here."

She taught us reading, writing, arithmetic, geography, and English with a spoonful of religion on the side. Religion is important to our family. She confirmed, out of all of us, I was the easiest to teach. I always graciously admit to her she was a great teacher!

Rachel moved to the big city on the East Coast to attend college. During her education, she was sent to other countries to do apprenticeships with some of the top names of the fashion industry. My sister has so much knowledge of the fashion world. It is amazing. What a fun job!

My brother Joseph and I will probably stay on the ranch. Our father has been grooming my brothers for a long time. Our parents have taught and guided my brothers to have the initiative, mechanical ability, physical strength, and interpersonal skills, along with patience, to run the ranch. On the other hand, this may have made them eager to pursue their career choices.

Our parents agreed Joe would run the ranch and keep it in our family for many generations to enjoy by grooming his children when he has them to help out and possibly run the ranch someday. While the others may find their happiness and gratification with different professions, they will always have the knowledge of the ranch. There are stipulations that we would all move back—one day commute when needed—to our careers, but that's an entirely different chapter of our lives. My siblings and I have no problem with that.

I am furthering my education to do the accounting with marketing skills so I can contract our beef with large companies to distribute to different grocery stores and restaurants across the United States. Joe spoke about it many times to my family; he confirmed I could talk a steer out of a blade of grass, that I have exceptional people skills, and I am good with numbers too.

Computer and Internet perusing are not Joe's strong suit. The triplets take care of that for now, although they have shown Joe how to order. Joe always exclaimed, "One thing at a time. I am not nor will I be too computer savvy. I am on the outdoor side of the ranch, not behind the desk." I am not sure which one of my brothers is smarter. I know they all have their own personal knowledge.

SIDEKICKS

*M*y brothers have beautiful log ranch homes with three bedrooms, two full baths, large fireplace, a wraparound porch, and two stables with a garage. Those are some of the highlights of their cute, quaint homes. Each one is unique with their interior style.

My brothers and sister are married. Joseph married Sarah, and they will be married for one year on New Year's Eve. They live on the top east corner of the ranch. Sarah is strong minded with shoulder-length dark-brown hair and large brown eyes. She is overly friendly and just as kind. She is not only book smart but good at everything. She is modest about it, not one to throw her intelligence around.

Sarah has a week, then she is done with college, and she will have her associate's degree as a website publisher. She is supersmart with computers and is close to completing the website for the ranch. She just needs the blessing of Father and her husband on some things before she sets it live. My father and Joe call her the website wizard. She will be taking care of cattle pickup from their home when the website goes live.

Sarah plans to set up other sites for customers and show them how to update their website, or they can sign a yearly contract with her. This will make them a client. Sarah works for the Grilling Post and set up a website for Gabby, Jacobs' wife. Sarah is the Grilling Post's reservation and wedding specialist. She books reservations for dinner and wedding receptions at the venue. This job is more like a wedding planner specialist for the Grilling Post. Sarah is the wedding-planning guru. That girl has contacts from bands to the person designing the wedding dress and everything in between. She loves this job as well.

Joshua married Ava. They have been married for a few months and have no children. They live on the far top west corner of the ranch. Both said their careers need to be successful before children come into the picture. Ava was shy when Joshua was dating her. She has short brown hair and large green eyes. She is also a doodler. These two could not be more fit for each other, like two peas in a pod. They will be a *corporation*, as Joshua calls it. She laughs when he says corporation because they have a long way to go before that happens. The business name of their company will be AJ Architecture. Ava has completed her last year of professional training for architectural school and has a project and thesis she is working on since the start of her last year, then she will have her doctorate in architecture. My hat is off to her! Doodle away, Ava!

Jacob married Gabrielle, Gabby for short. Jacob and Gabby will be the first to have children. They live on the lower west side of the ranch. Gabby has long, thick brown hair, just midback length, and large brown eyes. She is super-outgoing. She will be set with growing up in the family business. Her family will sign over the Grilling Post. It's a higher-end restaurant with delicious food. A selection of micro-brewed beer, mixed drinks, wines and champagne for special occasions, and reservations are required. The Grilling Post also has a beautiful large pavilion area with a kitchen they book for weddings all year round. She will be managing and running that full-time come January first.

Jeremiah married Sophia. They live on the east lower side of the ranch. They will probably go with their own private practice. Jeremiah and Sophia talk about how an office should run. That is what makes me think private instead of working for a group.

Sophia has beautiful midback-length red curly hair, the largest blue eyes like pools of water you've ever seen, and a midface of light freckles. She is the kindest soul and is always willing to overlook the bad qualities of a person to find the good in them. She will soon complete her nursing degree to help Jeremiah in cardiology specialty. We will see, but these two will be the last to take the children plunge.

My twin sister Rachel decided to marry an accountant she met when our father had a few business meetings with Jackson's father. Jackson and Rachel started dating soon after and were inseparable. My family knew they would marry. He works on Wall Street in New York City. His looks remind me of my father, a rugged cowboy of the accounting world. We only see Rachel and Jackson on holidays. They live in a beautiful penthouse in Manhattan, overlooking the Hudson River. I went to visit them a couple of times; city life is a busy life, very different than living on a ranch. I, on the other hand, love the open space of the ranch, my horse, and the solitude that comes with living on it with no one around for miles. The city is too crowded, too expensive. Between the two, Jackson and Rachel make excellent money, which makes living in Manhattan comfortable. My sister is a big wig in the fashion industry.

Rachel and Jackson have not started a family yet, not sure if they will. They enjoy skiing in the snow-covered mountains in Colorado and soaking up the sun on the beaches of Key West, which keeps them in their vacation solitude. I think in time, they will give parenting a chance. Not too sure they are in a hurry, although around the holidays, our parents talk about how nice it will be to see children running around the house. This statement puts an uncertain smile on all my siblings' faces. I know they are all a little hesitant because of our parents having multiple births.

I, on the other hand, need to get my selection process down. I have dated a few guys but none like Noah. Noah is the perfect gentleman—well-mannered, kind, so dedicated, not overly protective, loves to make me laugh, most times tries to work on my last nerve to make me angry—and he admits he has never seen me angry. I promise him, he doesn't want to! Noah's parents passed when he was seven years old. Noah was raised by his aunt Louise and uncle Eugene, whom he's hardly seen, so I guess you would say his au pair or nanny Fran raised him. At one point, his aunt and uncle were gone for six months. Fran took very good care of him.

Noah comes to the ranch to spend time with me. Noah and I ride the fence line to check for breaks, not to mention that we text each other all the time, but Noah and I both know college comes first. We met when I visited a college at the information table. We had lunch at the local café and went our separate ways. We did swap stories of growing up while sitting at the table in the café together. I told him how it is growing up in a large family, and he shared he was an only child and could only wish for brothers and sisters. We exchanged cell numbers, and now when he has time and I am free for a moment, we get together and do things.

I can't help but think what Noah will say when he meets my family, how confused he will be. Mother met him once, but everyone is always busy, and no one is ever at the ranch when he comes to visit. I did not tell him how duplicate my siblings and myself are; that may scare him, or maybe one day he will get those brothers and sister he never had. Makes me laugh inside to think about it! Noah has several degrees and is presently attending a school of business. I am hopeful this is the guy for me. Personally, I think my brothers and sister made perfect choices! I hope I will do the same.

RACHEL

My sister's horse Stally is buried under the large ponderosa pine tree on the hill overlooking the meadow of the first grazing pasture. Stally was diagnosed with Potomac fever caused by a bacteria. He put up a fight; thought we were good, then just passed in the night. This was a horrible time for my sister. Soon after the passing of Stally, my sister's college course in fashion design came to an end as well. She married Jackson and moved to Manhattan. I remember the week they came back from their honeymoon. She confessed, "It's really happening. I'm leaving the only family, town, and friends I have known all my life to move to the big city of New York."

I could hear the excitement and fright at the same time in Rachel's voice. I looked at her, and we both laughed. I kidded with her about the many friends she made in college and abroad when she traveled for education to other countries. "What about all those lifetime friends? I hope you don't forget about me that soon." I told her life has started for all of us when we were born. Her life of school and working on the ranch has come to an end, and now it is career, marriage, and children.

She insisted, "You sound like mother." She then rolled her eyes.

I told her, "You have to go." Grabbing her bags and walking to the stairs, I added, "Jackson is *not* sleeping in our room!"

Rachel wiped her tears, smiled, made a somewhat fist, and punched me in the arm. She helped me take her bags down the stairs to the veranda off the kitchen. Jackson was waiting for her there, speaking to our parents.

You can tell us apart easily if you take note of our personalities. For the most part, when Rachel is at the ranch, we dress a little the same. I am the more high-strung, happy, excitable one of the two of us. Rachel, on the other hand, is reigned in, so to speak. While Rachel was attending college, I think it put her mind in more of a perspective of a top high-class businesswoman. She has a *game face*. I have noticed over the years of Rachel living in Manhattan and working in the fashion world, it comes over her as soon as she steps out of her penthouse door onto the street. Rachel's game face reminds me of a "don't mess with me look." Rachel is super confident, and it shows. Maybe in that dog-eat-dog world on the East Coast, you need to acquire a look of confidence. Not sure. I call it her business look.

I met many of her friends who warned me about her—jokingly, of course—calling her a *pit bull* of the fashion industry. I did not know how to take that at first. I know it is a good quality and compliment. I must confess I've seen that side of her up close and personal. Not the fun side I know of Rachel at all; no way!

I met her right-hand man Caesar. He is her personal assistant. I think of him as an extension of her brain, extra memory, with reminders, encouraging words, and blurbs of fashion. Caesar is an average-sized man around the age of fifty, black spiked hair from the '80s, friendly but a little pushy. He has been in the fashion world for more years than dirt is old, he proclaims as he smiles and rushes me from in front of the camera to an area where I am out of the way. I would visit Rachel early fall after she moved to Manhattan. The older we get, the more interesting our lives become to each other.

Rachel is talking loudly to the models in front of the camera. She is chatting with the models to give them the look of having fun on the beach. "The young girls and women of all ages want to be you! They want to take that vacation to the beaches of warmer climates during these cooler months. Make them want your outfit! They will look as smashing as you in the swimsuits and cover-ups!" Rachel looks my way and smiles. "Great job, everyone!" Rachel is working with the next group of girls and a handful of guys to fix their outfits before they step in front of the camera. Rachel yells, "Kick the sand, throw the beach ball, and throw the pitcher of ice water at the guys! Now you got it!"

She barks at Caesar, "You need to check the calendar for the next photo shoot location. I want to be on the beaches and cliffs of Greece."

Caesar is to make this happen. Caesar quickly rushes around the room to find Rachel's laptop and brings up her calendar. Caesar is on the phone with someone and he is speaking Greek. My eyes widen, and I must be catching flies. *Amazing*, I thought. Caesar can speak a different language; I wonder how many languages he can speak. My sister told me he is an asset to her, keeps her on time and on schedule.

Caesar then looks my way and mentions lunch. Oh my, he is talking to me. Rachel is mentioning, "Caesar, make reservations at a restaurant near Wall

Street. We are meeting Jackson." She adds, "After lunch, Jackson needs to head into the office to grab some things. It will be easier and closer for Jackson if we plan lunch in that vicinity. It will be a working lunch, which may run a little late. Caesar, I need you to stop in about an hour after the original reservation."

Rachel grabs me by the hand, snatches her handbag off the desk, and we are out the door. We take the elevator to the street level. As we walk out of the tall skyscraper, I see a long white limo at the curb. The driver is a good-looking buff-sized tall young man in a black suit and tie, standing at the back passenger door by the curb. One can see his muscles through his suit.

He reaches at the back door of the limo, and the door opens. To my surprise, Jackson is inside. Jackson works from their Manhattan penthouse; he has been for quite some time now. I'm excited to see Jackson as I thought we would be meeting him at the restaurant.

Jackson, Rachel, and I are on our way to lunch. I don't know where we are eating, but I am sure it will be enjoyable. They have not taken me to a terrible place yet. They have had me try every different kind of food there is in their neighborhood. I can't wait to see where we will be eating today. "So this is how you guys get to see each other," I giggle. "I was wondering how things came together with both of you being so busy."

Jackson then assured me, "We try to catch time together during the day when we can. Also try spending time together when we are at home. Sometimes it works. Sometimes it doesn't. How are you today? I missed you this morning. Rachel's day starts so early. How are you enjoying the busy life of a fashion designer?"

I anxiously confirm, "I am enjoying my day."

He then told me, "Glad to hear, and the day is not over yet." Jackson smiles.

Jackson and Rachel are catching up on their day, letting each one know of the boundaries they faced for the first part of the day and what the rest of the day may hold, adding me into their conversation now and again. Jackson told me he just wants me to have a great time, and we will see sights before I have to leave to go home to Shimmering Meadow. They both smile and tell me they are glad I am here to visit. They love the break of family during their day and thanked me for coming.

As the limo pulls under the entrance canopy of the restaurant, Rachel is planning a shopping trip for after lunch. She states, "I will show you sights in the city between our shopping destinations. This will also give us sister time." Jackson is fine with that and adds, "I will keep working to get caught up on clients from work, and then we can watch a movie later when you both return to the penthouse."

We agree that sounds great. We enter the dimly lit restaurant and are escorted by the hostess Gia to a table by large windows near the back of the restaurant. As we are walking to our table, Gia asks while looking to Rachel and Jackson, "Will you be having sparkling water with the berries?" Jackson proceeds to say, "Yes, thank you, Gia. Rebekah, what would you like to drink?"

I reply, "Water is fine. Thank you." Gia leaves our table to get our drinks.

Jackson proceeds to say, "This restaurant is where we had our first official date. I took the liberty to order our lunch ahead of time so your business lunch can start on time. I hope you don't mind." Jackson looks to both of us and kisses Rachel.

"No, that's fine. Thank you," Rachel replies.

Our food arrives. It's shrimp vegetable fettuccine Alfredo with seasoned asparagus, zucchini, and tiny sprinkle of yellow squash, lunch portion size, of course.

I tell Jackson, "This looks delicious, too pretty to eat." Jackson smiles. The waiter Enzo asks, "Is there anything else you need?"

Jackson looks to Rachel and I, "No, Enzo. I think we have everything. Thank you." Jackson slips him a fifty. Enzo smiles. "Thank you." Enzo leaves our table, and I see him check on others in his path as he makes his way back to the kitchen.

Jackson and Rachel chat a little more about their day, vacation, and coming to the ranch for thanksgiving.

We are finished eating, Jackson is saying good bye to us. I see the hostess Gia walking toward our table with Caesar. We are finished eating, and Jackson is getting ready to leave. Caesar is speaking to the host of the restaurant as they are walking toward our table.

The waiter brings our caramel chocolate espressos, and Jackson tells Caesar not to work Rachel too hard. The laptops are out on the table with a beggar's purse appetizer that is followed by a bagel and lox sandwich for Caesar.

Caesar is going over some details about Rachel's photo shoot she wanted to schedule. He is going over dates and tells Rachel he will inform the crew and her model selection as well. Caesar says his goodbyes, and they are done. The business part of this lunch is over. We walk out of the restaurant, and the limo is waiting to pick us up. We take the limo to Macy's, Tiffany's and a quick grocery list is sent to the grocery store to be delivered to the penthouse. Rachel looks to me and asks, "How does Chinese sound for later this evening while we watch a movie?"

I agree, "Sounds good." Rachel tells me this will be delivered by the time we are ready to watch the movie. I tell her, "Straying from the list puts a spin on dinner. I like spontaneous. Spontaneous is exciting!"

Life in the city moves so fast. Everything is too dependent on others. It seems like I take the little things for granted, like driving to the grocery store. I am glad I go back to the ranch in a few days. I would not like to drive through New York, not at all. I miss the quiet and driving back home. We are back at the penthouse, and I am in the shower, thinking about leaving in a few days to get back to the ranch. I miss Jackson and Rachel already. Thanksgiving cannot come soon enough.

I find myself lured to the bar between the living room and the kitchen. Jackson is in the living room, looking for a movie. Rachel is talking a mile a minute, wiping off the groceries and putting them away. I ask her what the purpose of grocery shopping was if the day after tomorrow we all will be leaving—I to go home, she and Jackson to Colorado.

She admits Caesar stays at their penthouse to catsit Jinx, who has anxiety. I look at her in bewilderment. "Anxiety? Why? Your cat has a great life." I look to Rachel with disbelief; I want to take the cat home with me.

Rachel explains that since the cat was alone for a few months after she got her, it developed anxiety coming from a large litter and being the runt of the litter. I interrupt her and ask if I can take the cat home with me. She then says, "Well, I will miss her, but I am never home. I thought getting a cat would make it easier for me not to be homesick for the ranch. I will think about it."

Jackson chimes in, "I feel terrible for the cat. I have her with me all day. I feed her while I eat, and most times, I sit on the sofa in hopes she will feel comforted I am with her. I have her lay on my lap, or I move to the sofa so she has more room to lie next to me so she knows I am not going anywhere. It is hard for her. We just can't bring ourselves to give her away."

Jackson is petting the cat. Rachel adds, "Jinx is six years old. We got her after we first moved in. I tried to do without animals, not wanting to get attached but just could not do it."

I tell Rachel the cat is a Ragdoll. She has the qualities and personality of a dog—loyal, true to their owner. I would guess she needs to have someone with her all the time. "Please rethink my taking her with me. I can watch her for you. She can stay in our old room with me."

Rachel insists I check out the magazine on the counter. I flip through the mail to find the magazine she is speaking of under a realtor envelope and some baby magazines. Hmm…she then states, "If you can find the magazine in all that junk mail."

I place things to the side on the counter and page through the magazine. A hand comes across the bar to the magazine with a slap. "Hold that page!" Rachel then grinned. "What do ya think? That is a wedding dress I designed when I was in high school that I scribbled on a napkin during lunch. I have four brides across the country in all directions for this dress. I love when the bride e-mails the company and says they need a dress. It is such a wonderful feeling!"

I confusingly whisper, "When did you get into wedding dresses?" She usually designs summer clothes. Swimsuits and cover-ups are big with her— summer dresses, things like that.

She then tells me, "I design a wedding dress at least once a year. I scribble one together throwing in some intricate notions, somewhat risky low-cuts and slits, however, keeping the dress elegant and tasteful. They are high end and very pricey."

Rachel was always interested in wedding attire and drew wedding dresses growing up. My parents thought for the longest time this is what she would be designing when she started in the fashion industry. Rachel blurted, "I will soon have a chance to work from home as a remote account specialist. This position will be offered to me soon." She babbles on about how she will be a freelance designer of wedding dresses. She proceeds to tell me how things will work. The client contacts her with requests for the dress design she has already sketched. The office, in turn, contacts Rachel to design and work with them. This process takes a while. The design of the wedding gown will go back and forth from Rachel to the client multiple times until the perfect dress is visualized.

Rachel does a 360 during the conversation and is asking about everyone back home. We started this conversation when I was picked up at the airport on Sunday afternoon; it is now Wednesday evening. So I begin to tell Rachel what has been happening, which is not much really. I finish, and Rachel tells Jackson and me she is going for a shower. It is amazing how her mind is all over the place; Mother said Rachel's mind is constantly going, thinking, busy. She will start a sentence or continue a conversation that was started anywhere from two minutes ago to a week ago. I am glad to see she is still the same old Rachel. I wonder if she does this at work, although I think she does it because of the stress at work.

The doorman, Matt, buzzes the penthouse suite, and Jackson answers. Matt notifies Jackson dinner has been left with him by the Chinese delivery person. Jackson tells Matt, "I will be right down!" Jackson looks my way, assures me he will be right back, as he takes the elevator down to the lobby. I watch the monitor by the kitchen bar that is hooked to a few cameras, one in the elevator, one in the lobby entrance, and another in the opposite side of the living room of the penthouse focused on the elevator. I see Matt waiting at the elevator with the bags.

In no time at all, the elevator door opens, and Jackson is back. He places the food on the island in the kitchen and tells me to help myself as he hands me a plate. Rachel comes out to the kitchen with her hair in a towel. Rachel, dressed in her PJs, grabs a plate and joins us on the comfortable sofa. We are watching a movie Jackson found on the flat screen. It was a two-hour edge-of-your-seat cliff-hanger movie. Action-packed with explosions, the movie has five minutes left, and Rachel has fallen asleep. I take her empty plate from her hand. Jackson hands me his as the credits are rolling on the screen. I place them in the dishwasher, put the leftovers away, and say my good nights as Jackson carries Rachel up the stairs and into their room, which has a balcony overlooking the downstairs. I am glad I took a shower earlier because I am not sure what they have planned for me tomorrow. This way, I will be ready.

I spent the next two days with both of them showing me New York sights. I like to see them but miss being home on the ranch. It is just so crowded and noisy. We take the limo to all the cool attractions. We visited the Empire State Building, then took the boat to Ellis Island where we walked around and visited the Statue of Liberty. We walked through Central Park, and I also purchased some cheap items from shady people on the streets dressed in trench coats as others lured us to places in the alleys for knock-off purses and other items. We saw the cowboy in Times Square strumming on his guitar. We then grabbed a bite to eat and went back to the penthouse.

When we get to the penthouse, I say, "I cannot believe how exhausted I am from walking and interacting with strangers, purchasing and carrying the bags because we are all hard workers. A day like today should not have made us feel like this." I laugh and drop to the couch.

It is my last night here, and Jackson orders Italian food for delivery. Jackson says, "We do cook, but we want to spend time with you, so I hope you don't mind us ordering in while you're here."

I tell him, "Not at all. Ordering out is fine."

We eat, clean up, chat for a while and knowing we need to catch our flight early tomorrow; we say our good nights and turn in.

Morning is here before ya know it. I make sure I have everything packed, inspecting the room and bathroom I used while I stayed. The penthouse is quiet with the exception of Rachel and Jackson's running around upstairs, getting things together as well. They yell to me from upstairs and ask if I am up. I yell to them and kiddingly tell them I will be staying another week. They laugh, and say, "Of course you are!"

They come down the stairs all loaded down with their bags like a stampede. I look at them in bewilderment. "You two staying for a month?" As I help them get the bags to the floor, I add, "Are you only allowed to come down the stairs one time?"

They laugh and tell me, "We do this all the time. It's like a game between us. Although we over-pack, we tell each other we don't have all that much."

"Okay," I say as I laugh at both of them. "I have this little duffel bag of clothes. You have six bags each. How do they allow all of that on the plane?"

Jackson now tells me they will be flying on the company jet.

"So we will be going to the airport together?" I confirm.

"Yes. We got you a direct flight home," Rachel explains.

We drive to the airport, and the limo took us to a different spot where we were right at a jet. I help them get their bags on the jet. Jackson grabs my bag. I hold my hand out to grab it, and he asks me if I want it with us on the top or in the underside?

"Oh, what? Did I say that out loud?" My eyes are widened, and I am looking at both of them. "I am flying with you?" I excitedly reply.

Jackson exclaims, "Rachel told you your flight was direct." He smiles and helps me on board.

We got seated, and the waiter notified us what breakfast held for us, eggs any way we wanted them, including omelets. The waiter went on to offer French toast with cinnamon and vanilla sprinkled with powdered sugar, regular or blueberry pancakes topped with a fruit glaze, and a side of fresh fruit with more than enough choices of drinks from bottled water to mocha coffees and juices. I had a delicious breakfast, watched a half-hour movie, and had a snack of fruit with some yogurt ice cream for lunch, and now we were landing. We said our goodbyes, hugged, and agreed we would see each other on Thanksgiving. I thanked them for the ride in the jet.

There was a car waiting at the side of the jet and the driver drove me to my jeep. Off I was to Shimmering Meadow, it will be good to be back. On the drive to the ranch, I thought of all the fun I had with Rachel and Jackson, how exciting to ride in their private jet. "Wait, their private jet?" I need to confirm that with Rachel after their trip to Colorado.

THE PHONE CALL

It is late fall. I make my way downstairs from my room. As I look through the screen door of the living room, I see my brothers with their drones, which they use to check on the cattle. They have to keep their eye out for wolves, coyotes, mountain lions, and grizzlies. These wild animals are always lurking around in the chance they could get a free meal.

My brothers notify me the cattle are only around the bend from the house, their horses tied up at the post near the house in case they need to take a quick trip before heading out to the cattle later in the evening. While I am out chatting with my brothers, I hear the phone. My mother answers; it sounds like she is talking to Rachel. I run in through the living room to the kitchen to say hello. It was a quick, short call; by the time I reach my mother, the call had ended.

Mother confirms Rachael and Jackson will be at the ranch in a few days to spend a week with the family over the Thanksgiving holiday. I can't believe Thanksgiving is this Thursday. They will fly in and rent a car, as always. I wonder if they are bringing their jet or if they are taking a commercial flight first class. I need to ask her about the jet when they get here. I got too busy over the past months with everything at the ranch, I did not get to ask her when we spoke. No biggie. We look forward to their visit as we don't see them with the exception of the holidays. They call more than they visit because their careers keep them busy.

I noticed Mother sitting at the kitchen counter with her notepad and pen, making a grocery list. I tell Mother I need to do errands for Father and Joe in town tomorrow, and I can pick up her groceries if she'd like. Mother then informs me while she is writing down and into the middle of her page, "Yes, I would like if you could pick up the groceries. We will need a thirty-pound turkey."

I tell mother to place the list on the table with my keys, and I will take care of that tomorrow. I look over her shoulder to see the ingredients for the most amazing Thanksgiving dinner ever! I can taste the food just looking at the list. Mother's ingredients for her candied sweet potatoes with dark-brown sugar and marshmallows are the most delicious I have ever tasted. Then there's her thirty-pound turkey basted in its own juice, breast down, which keeps the breast meat moist. Mother stuffs the filling into the turkey which gives it a wonderful flavor. Sarah does the potato filling and the honey-baked ham. Sarah sprinkles dark-brown sugar on top after covering the ham with Persephinie's honey that she harvests from her bees in the summer. Persephinie is a close friend of Ava. After the dark-brown sugar, Sarah places pineapple rings on top of the ham with cherries placed in the centers. Mother says it is all in the presentation. I can taste it already. It is enough to put a diabetic into a seizure, but I love my sugar.

Then there is the large bowl of sour creamed, garlic mashed potatoes. Mother makes some of our freshly frozen vegetables picked from our garden this past summer. Sophia takes the juice from the turkey and places it on top of the potato filling. She also takes the broth from both the ham and the turkey and makes gravies. I am so hungry just looking at this list. I am so ready for Thanksgiving dinner!

I walk into the living room. My father is sitting in his chair, reading the paper, and listening to the news on the television. I ask if there is anything interesting in the newspaper. Father looks over the newspaper to confirm, "Everything in the paper is interesting." He smiles, flips the paper. I hear him remark, "Rebekah, would you like the funny page as you read when you were younger?" I hear him chuckle.

"No, Father, I will look at the stock page when you are done."

Joe is shuffling through papers at the desk. Talking to my father, Joe speaks of the cattle contract for the cattle pickup tomorrow at 5:00 a.m. as Joe keeps searching. Father calmly places the newspaper in his lap. Looking over his glasses at Joe, he asks about the paper Joe had on the scanner yesterday.

Joe wanted to look over the contract one more time before scanning and e-mailing it to the buyer. Joe finds the contract right where he let it—in the scanner, unscanned. Joe then looks at Father, smiles, and thanks him for his help. Joe pulls the chair out from the desk and reviews the contract, reading it, making sure things are in order before scanning. Joe asks Father if he would like to look it over as well.

Father informed Joe, "I already checked it earlier and placed it back in the scanner. I checked the sent area of the e-mails to make sure you did not send it before I reviewed it." With a smile, Father lifts the paper and begins to read again.

Joe is listening to Father, then places the contract facedown once again in the scanner. "I thought I would review it once more before forwarding it to the buyers. Thank you for checking it over." Joe scans the contract then attaches it to the buyer's e-mail with a brief note and address to the ranch. Joe received a confirmation of the e-mail, now Joe can relax.

Joe walks in the room where Father is sitting and plops in a recliner next to Father as he is chatting about the cattle pickup. I look to my father to find him still with his head in the newspaper, nodding his head to every word Joe is saying. My father finally puts the paper down again, probably for the last time. I say that because he is folding the newspaper and placing it on the table between Joe and himself. I reach and snag the newspaper before Joe takes it. I need to see the price cattle are going for these days, and then I will place it back on the table.

They are in deep conversation about the website Sarah is working on for the ranch. Joe has a pen, and he is jotting down some things that are crucial to the site. The information that needs to be placed on the website is about the quality of the cattle. Our ranch has raised Simmental, Charolais, Aberdeen Angus, and Black Angus since my parents started this ranch. Sarah is adding pictures of the different types of cattle on the website, and she holds emphasis on the location as well as one hundred thousand acres of the most plush green fields north of the Grizzlies Eye Mountain and south of the Grizzly Back Falls, Wyoming.

Joe's wife, Sarah, comes through the kitchen door and into the living room like a house on fire, so giddy and excitable, bouncing off the walls. She sits on the floor next to Joe and asks if Rachael called. Joe mentioned Mother did get a call from Rachel. Rachel called to confirm they will be arriving Wednesday before Thanksgiving. That's four days from now. Sarah smiles this cute but sneaky smile, and we are all wondering what she is hiding.

Sarah is a trap when it comes to secrets. Sarah will keep the secret but throw some questions around and flirt with the situation, never to reveal what she was told. We know nothing. On the other hand, we all know Sarah knows something. It's like a cat-and-mouse game with her. This is one of the qualities I love about my sister-in-law!

The entrance of Sarah has my mother finding her way to the living room. Father is looking at Sarah, asking her if there is something we should know. Before he has his question out, she immediately says, "Nothing!" with the biggest I-know-something smile ever! We all wonder what news Rachael and Jackson will share. Our parents think Jackson probably got a raise. Rachael may have an opportunity to work with another famous designer, and I do remember Rachel mentioning a position that was coming up, although I'm not sure that is it. I'm guessing she will be jet setting to fly off to another exotic beach to do the photo shoot. We will have to wait and see. I am glad it is only a few days away, so we will soon find out what secret Sarah is hiding.

In the meantime, I need to get Mother back to the kitchen to make a list of cookies, cakes, and pies we will be making. This is something all the girls do together the night before the holidays. Mother reaches in the refrigerator and pulls a few bowls of pie fillings she has started to mix, saying she wants to get a jump on things. The pie filling flavors are cherry, blueberry, apple, peach, and strawberry—all picked from our fruit orchard this past year.

While Mother and I are busy, Sarah pulls a chair out from the side of the table, grabs a stick of butter and the container of flour. She starts to prepare the pie pans for the piecrust. Sarah mixes the piecrust and takes it to the floured table to roll out to place in the piedishes. She then places the crust over each pie plate, arranging by pressing the crust into the pan, and then starts to trim around the edges. She has eight pie pans with crusts ready to pour the filling and top some with the lattice and the others with crumbs.

Mother follows right after to pour all the mixtures of different fillings in each prepared crust, as Sarah places crumbs on some pies and lattice on the remaining pies. Mother makes two of each flavor.

While the pies are being placed in the ovens, Mother asks, "Sarah, do you need anything from town tomorrow? Rebekah is running in to the feed mill for supplies and stock food mix."

Sarah asks eagerly, "Could I travel along as I have something I need to do."

I told Sarah I was taking the truck with the trailer because I need to pick up grain, hay and straw, new grooming brushes for the horses, and a prescription of vaccinations for the calves. I have a list as long as my arm, then I need to stop by the grocery store for the Thanksgiving feast. Sarah says, "I can help with the grocery list by e-mailing the list to the store so they can get it ready for us to pick up."

I hand her my laptop and the list of groceries. Sarah moves to the other end of our large dining room table and starts completing the information to open an account, then tapping out the list of groceries Mother needs on the grocery stores website, she is telling me this will be ready tomorrow when we are ready to leave town. I say, "Wow, that just saved us two hours. When we get to the feed mill, I just need to back the trailer at the loading dock. Joe called in our order for the livestock. Then I need to pick out the brushes for the horses and grab the vaccinations from the veterinarian's office. What do you need?"

Sarah told us she wants to stop by the salon on the west side of town. She said, "Lindra has openings if you would like to join me. The grocery shopping is done. We can grab a chair at the salon. We just have to swing by the grocery store to pick up the order when we are done."

I said, "That's great! I was thinking of getting my hair cut."

Mother then said, "I wish I was caught up on things I have to do so I could tag along. I would like my roots colored before Rachael and Jackson arrive in four days."

Sarah said, "Well, that's settled. You are going along!"

I looked at Mother and Sarah. "We need to get busy! Mother, what do you need us to do?"

Sarah grabs her cell phone and makes two more appointments with two stylists for Mother and me. She then said, "You should have an appointment in a few—"

As she was going to say *minutes*, her cell phone let out the notification sound, and an appointment with two stylists were made. She notifies us we are booked. Mother and I could not believe how fast that happened.

We helped Mother with more than she wanted to do. I went up to my room to get it straightened up for the arrival of Jackson and Rachael since they will be sleeping on Rachel's side of my room. Holidays are a lot of work but so much fun, and it is nice to have family home. All my siblings come home with my sibling-in-laws and stay in their old rooms.

We have a busy, full house for five days, if not more. Everyone arrives the day before the holiday. Father lights a fire in the fireplace. Mother rounds up all the girls to bake cookies and catch up. Every Thanksgiving Day, we saddle up the horses and take a family ride. On the third night after Thanksgiving, we put up our Christmas decorations as a family. The men do the outside; we gals do the inside. My father puts the ten-foot artificial tree in the living room by the fireplace, ready to decorate. Mother does not like real trees; they drop needles and dry up quickly.

Sarah and Joe are staying at the house this evening since everyone will be going separate ways tomorrow. Jeremiah, Joshua, and Jacob are out camping with half the herd near the meadow. Joe will join them sometime tomorrow to help bring them in to the barn. I have to ride out to them when I get back from town to give them the vaccinations for the calves. It is easier to vaccinate them while they are in the field.

I make my way to the kitchen and grab cereal and a glass of milk. I sit at the table, listening to the chatter in the living room among my parents, Joe, and Sarah. I finish my cereal and say my good nights to everyone, hugging Mother and Father. I tell them, "4:00 a.m. comes pretty early, so I am turning in. Today went so fast!"

I make my way to my room to do an hour of Internet work for a few college classes then close my laptop and slide into my bed. I listen, instead of falling asleep, to the sound of my family's voices downstairs, laughing, being giddy, and talking about the Thanksgiving holiday. I can't sleep thinking of the exciting news that my sister and her husband have to tell us. Being a twin, I wonder about that "twin power" everyone talks about. I need to sleep. My chores need to be done before I leave with my mother and Sarah tomorrow. I yawn. I see my clock. It says 11:30 p.m., and...the alarm goes off. Wow! I just shut my eyes. I spring from my bed, race to the bathroom, take a shower to get awake, brush my teeth, and off to the barn to do my chores.

I walk off the porch, go across the yard to the barn, and I see the tractor trailer truck has arrived. My father and Joe were in the kitchen with a coffee, getting into their boots. The tractor trailer is backing up to the loading area to collect cattle for market. I wave to them and tell them my father and Joe are on their way.

I start my chores: let twelve horses out to pasture, muck the fifteen stables, run fresh water to the pasture, dust the stables with sawdust, feed the chickens, collect eggs, feed the kitties, and I am done. That was not bad.

I pass through the kitchen and smell the roast in the oven for dinner tonight. Mother always adds ten pounds of diced potatoes, two bags of baby carrots, and four bags of frozen peas. The roaster with the three large roasts and all those veggies make a delicious one-pot meal. Mother was up and getting ready for the day. I cannot wait for dinner; it smells great! I take my very-much-needed shower, get dressed, throw makeup on, hair back in a ponytail, then head back to the kitchen. I need to start breakfast for us girls before we have to leave for our morning in town.

I hear Mother and Sarah stirring. I smell bacon, eggs, and toast, and I grab my hot chocolate from the counter. I set the table for us; we eat and chat about what the day holds for us in town. I walk to the truck at the barn. Joe tells me everything is good with the trailer and not to forget to take the wide turns as he giggles and says, "Father don't want no stop signs coming back to the ranch."

I tell him, "Thanks for the vote of confidence," and I'm off to the house to pick up Mother and Sarah.

We leave the ranch and in twenty minutes reach the feed mill. My father's childhood friend Jim meets us as we pull into the lot. Jim has owned the feed mill for well over thirty-five years. I ask Jim if I should back the trailer to the dock. Jim says to pull it to the right of the blue truck, and he will back the trailer to the feed mill dock. It is 7:30 a.m. Jim tells me, "When the truck is loaded, I will text you. It should take about two hours at the most. Then I will have them move the truck to the pickup area for you. Just take your time. Have a nice morning."

I thank Jim and tell him I will await his text.

Sarah, Mother, and I started our brisk but sunny walk two blocks to the salon. We walked past the park, post office, bakery, and a cute little strip mall with a fountain they finished this past summer. The fountain was already winterized with a heavy canvas covering. The circle bed was blanketed with beautiful straw, fall-colored flowers surrounding it. A few decorative short droopy pine trees graced the boarder of the garden. "Looks beautiful even in the fall," I excitedly tell Mother and Sarah.

As we passed the bakery, it smelled sweet and delicious. Mother was wondering about stepping into the bakery on our way back to order a tray of cookies decorated for fall. "It is possible if the salon appointments don't take too long," Sarah told Mother. "They have really good pumpkin pies."

We reach the salon and are seated in our chairs at the same time. Mother tells her beautician Meg she would like her roots done. I tell my beautician Sy I need my hair cut. I close my eyes and just listen to the chatting around me. Sarah is like a Chatty Cathy doll. The beautician is a friend of Sarah from Deadwood, South Dakota, and owns the salon. Sarah lived in Deadwood when she was growing up. Later, Sarah's parents moved to Bear Creek. Bear Creek is where my brother met her; they started dating, and, well, you know the rest.

The salon has ten chairs, with a washbowl at every station, and the girls are busy! Everyone is supernice. Mother is talking about our holiday plans, and Sarah is rattling on about recipes. Sarah is a great cook. She is a smart cook, or else, my brother Joe would be gaining weight like crazy. I tell everyone Sarah cooks smart meals. I hear Sarah's friend Lindra say she heard Rachel and Jackson are coming home. Hmm, it's the way Lindra said it. Sarah is talking softer. I cannot hear what she is saying; my chair spins and faces mother. Mother did not hear Lindra or Sarah. Now the topic is kids. When are Joe and Sarah having them?

Okay, now my eyes go shut again, and I am relaxed. I find myself waking up with a perfect haircut! Everyone is done, paid, tipped, and ready to go. The time is 9:30 a.m. Perfect! I thought I will soon be getting a text from Jim, and there is the text message alert.

I tell Mother I just got the text from Jim. Mother is anxious about getting back to the feed mill. Sarah and I tell her we are stopping at the bakery first. "Mother, Jim told me they would park the truck at the pickup area. The truck and trailer are not in anyone's way there. We are stopping at Brittney's Bakery because we are shopping sweets. Who doesn't have time for sugar?"

Mother and Sarah laugh. Sarah says, "It's a wonder your teeth don't fall out, although that may explain why you are high-strung and hyper as you are, Rebekah."

Mother grabs a small tray of cookies of her choice and a pumpkin pie. Brittney tells mother, "Mrs. Sawyer, if you need anything, you just call. We always have time for you."

Mother smiles and thanks Brittney. Mother tells Brittney, "I will call the bakery tomorrow if these passed the Joe test for taste."

Brittney smiles, wishing us a happy Thanksgiving, and she will await a call from Mother.

As we walk back to the feed mill, Mother mentions she had a great time today. Just to get away from the holiday things she has to do for a few moments at the house is a great break in her day. Mother thanked us for helping, as we always do, and getting her caught up with cleaning.

We reach the feed mill, and I grab the brushes I need for the horses. I stop by the veterinarian pharmacy to grab the vaccines then to Jim's office to pay the bill for the feed and other things they loaded. I see Jim sitting at his desk, legs crossed, foot swinging, talking on his phone. Jim is talking to my father about Rachel and Jackson. He mentioned to my father that I am standing in his office; he guesses to pay the bill.

They say their goodbyes. Jim uncrosses his legs, now on his feet, hangs up the phone, and looks my direction. "Your hair, you got it cut," Jim says.

I tell him, "Yes, I wanted something different. My father told you Rachael and Jackson called and will be coming home?"

Jim says, "Yes, your father said they called to confirm they would be in. I am guessing in three days."

"Yes," I tell Jim. I ask him how much for the items I had to pick up.

Jim confirms, "Joe already paid it."

I tell him thanks for all his help, and off to the grocery store we go.

On our way to the store, Sarah signs into the grocery website account she set up. Mother hands her the bank card from my parents' account.

Sarah pays for the groceries, and with my mother's approval, the card is stored securely on the stores site for future purchases. We pull up to the curb. Sarah jumps out, opens the tailgate to the truck, flashes her cell phone for confirmation, groceries are loaded by the store attendant, and we are on our way home. I almost miss waiting around and walking up and down the aisles of the grocery store. Nah, no I don't! Hahaha!

Mother and Sarah are talking about vacuuming and dust mopping the entire first floor of the house. She is asking Sarah if we should wax the wood floors as they are making a game plan: windows, bathrooms, and dining room to get the serving counters ready; Wednesday night, preset the dinner table.

We pull into Shimmering Meadow. I drop Sarah and Mother off at the house, take the truck and trailer to the barn so the boys can unload the trailer. I back it in under the barn on the second floor. I get it unhooked and off to the house to unload the many bags of groceries. Sarah, Mother, and I put the groceries away. I put the turkey in a large pot of water in the walk-in cooler off the kitchen.

We sit in the kitchen at the counter. Sarah alerts Mother, "The coffee is ready!"

I tell them, "Hold my hot chocolate."

Mother and Sarah are talking of today's adventure, while I take the vaccinations out to the cattle grazing area. I should not be long. Father told me the boys, cattle, and collies are close to the house just around the bend in the meadow. I saddle up Duchess and take sandwiches Mother made with a thermos of coffee and a cookie for each one of them.

I am back forty-five minutes later, just in time to help in the house. Sarah and I clean the attic like a tornado in a windstorm. All the linens are cleaned, and we are placing them back on the beds. The penthouse suite is spotless and ready for our family.

I tell Sarah that Ava, Gabby, and Sophia arrive tomorrow from the far corners of the ranch, and they are going to help clean the rest of the house. Mother told everyone to grab a plate and get something to eat. "The roast is ready!" Everyone filters through into the living room after filling their dinner plate with food. Mother announces, "I have something I would like you to try when you are done with your dinner so save some room."

We take our plate to the dishwasher after eating. All of us gather in the living room, waiting to try those cookies Mother purchased earlier today at the bakery along with a slither of pie.

I am going to miss baking cookies with my sisters if these cookies turn out to be better than our family recipes. The quality time spent in my mother's kitchen is valued by all us girls. The stories and laughing like a bunch of schoolgirls are memorable for all of us. Mother tells us stories of her and Father in their younger days courting. Then my sisters-in-law jump in and share their stories of how the boys chased them, lines they used (really silly stuff), how awkward my brothers were talking to girls for the first time.

Mother has the small sample tray, and she goes around the room. Everyone takes a cookie as I sit there waiting for them to taste it. Father and Joe finally take a bite of their cookie, then they take another bite and another bite. I am actually wondering if our father likes the cookies. Neither one said they did or did not like them. Father guesses the cookies are all right. Joe is not a fan. So it looks like the cookie tradition still reigns in our family the night before every holiday. Perfect! We all hang out in the living room, talking about Rachel and Jackson.

I work my way up the stairs to my room, with my sister on my mind. If something was wrong, she would be here without a call, so it can't be life-threatening. I must wait two more days. Tomorrow I have to exercise the horses; that will be an all-day job. Then I will help clean up the living room, dining room, and kitchen.

I turn on my laptop to finish the last paragraph of my report for one of my online classes. I want to submit this tonight, then I won't have to do anything until a week after Thanksgiving. I turn my lamp off, and I am done! I hear everyone say their good nights as we are all turning in for the night. I fall asleep to the thoughts of Rachel and their news.

I wake up without the alarm, and the time is 3:30 a.m. My game plan for the barn is to groom the horses first, clean their hooves, then place them one at a time in the pasture for some exercise. Father told me I did not have to saddle up to exercise the horses since the family will take a trip out into the cattle grazing pasture Wednesday after Rachel and Jackson arrive. I'm up and walking out to the barn, moving swiftly and getting my chores completed. I am done in a few hours.

I go back to the house, take a shower, then to the living room to clean. I work my way down the stairs to have a little breakfast. I see the light on at the desk in the office area of the living room, and my father is sitting at the desk, looking at the computer. I walk around the back of his desk, asking if he is purchasing something online. He quickly minimizes the screen into the bar at the bottom of the monitor and tells me he is online Christmas shopping for Mother. I tell him Christmas is only a month away. My father is always the first one done Christmas shopping.

Father giggles; he lets me in on a little secret. "Yeah, I know, Rebekah. I ran out of time and have to find time now."

I let him know if he needs help to surf the Internet or if I need to pick anything up for him, all he has to do is ask. Father thanks me and tells me he will definitely let me know if I have to do anything for him.

As I make my way to the kitchen, I tell Father I fed the livestock. He tells me he was going to go to the barn after breakfast. Now he can relax. Our kitchen is so busy when everyone is home. I know mother will be up soon, so I will start breakfast. The timer just clicked on the coffeepot, and is starting to brew. I have the potatoes, onions, and bacon frying. Mother hugs me and says good morning as she takes over making breakfast.

The smell of breakfast always brings everyone from all directions of the house to the kitchen. Father walks by me and I hand him a cup of coffee. I serve Joe, Sarah, and Mother their coffee, and I ask what kind of eggs they would like.

I hear the kitchen door open, and Ava, Gabby, and Sophia have arrived. They grab a coffee, which finishes the pot, and Ava starts brewing another pot.

Mother tells me the blueberries are in the freezer. "Place the blueberries in hot water in the sink for a bit, and then we can fold them into the pancake batter."

I get the blueberries for mother and do as she says. Mother soon has breakfast ready.

We stand at the table, holding hands. Father says a prayer: "Father, we thank you for this food we are about to eat. We thank you for family, friends, happiness, life, strength, and our good health. We ask that you keep our family and others safe this holiday season and always. We ask that you bless everyone and give knowledge to the ones who need it to help others. We ask in Jesus's name," and we all say, "Amen."

As we sit down to breakfast, Father starts by speaking about the current news on the radio, television or newspaper he has read or heard. Mother is talking to us girls about the foods we have to prepare and the cleaning that is left to do before the holiday is here.

We place the dishes in the dishwasher, and Mother asks Sophia to start mixing the potato filling and bread filling. I change the water on the turkey and put it back in the walk-in cooler. Ava, Sarah, Gabby, and I continue cleaning the dining room and living room. We finish presetting the table and the serving counters in the dining room so we do not have to do it tomorrow night when Jackson and Rachel come.

We return to the kitchen in a few hours to discuss more of what needs to be done and if anyone will be trying any new recipes for the Thanksgiving dinner. Sarah takes two bowls from the cooler to finish the homemade cranberry sauce; she is telling Mother she has found a new recipe for the cranberry sauce and cannot wait for everyone to try it. Mother asks if it is from her friend in Hawaii. Sarah said, "Yes. The ingredients are orange juice, orange liqueur, or I could use cherry brandy as an option instead of the liqueur. I always use fresh cranberries."

I ask, "Doesn't it taste too orangey?"

Sarah blurted out with a giggle, "No, it tastes just right."

Gabby gets up from the stool to clean the coffeepot they emptied for the third time today. Gabby passes the window in the kitchen and sees the boys with the cattle coming to the pasture at the barn. Gabby puts her left arm around Ava and right arm around Sarah—and with a big smile—to announce to everyone, "Guess what, girls, the holiday is here! All the boys are home from the drive!"

Jacob, Joshua, and Jeremiah brought the cattle to the barn, where they will stay for the next few months until spring thaw then the cattle will go back out to the grazing fields to eat grass. My brothers are in the barn for a few hours with the cattle, getting them watered and fed. It takes some time to feed five hundred plus cattle.

After the cattle are put away for safekeeping, my brothers hit the showers. Sarah grabs all the clothing and puts it in the washer.

Father throws wood into the fireplace to keep the fire going. Our family sits on the oversized wrap-around sofa in the living room, relaxing, talking about Jackson and Rachel's arrival tomorrow at noon. With every word, I keep watching Sarah. Her wide eyes look like she is bursting with information. Joe sees her and says, "Ya know, I cannot wait for Jackson and Rachel to arrive." He squeezes Sarah; they both smile.

Mother is sitting in the corner, reading her book, dozing off as her book slides off her hands and into her lap. She is fast asleep. Father notices and gently lays a blanket over her. Father changes the conversation to the ride he will take us on tomorrow. All I know is I need to bring my slicker as it may be a little chilly riding. Father is talking about a forty-five-minute ride, so I am guessing we are going out to the meadow, or we could go forty-five minutes in another direction. I am not sure, so I will have to wait until tomorrow.

The lasagna smells so good. We are all talking about how hungry we are and that Mother has not made this dish in a while. Mother calls us to the kitchen to grab a plate, salad, a drink of our choice, then off to the living room we go. We are all cozied up to the fire again to finish chatting. Mother is complimented on her delicious meal.

Mother wants to know what we think about stromboli, pizza, subs, and salad for tomorrow from Pizza Stone. Ava loves that place. They deliver, so that will work for us.

Gabby suggested we take the extra cookies to the church for the luncheon on Sunday. Sophia contacted the lady in charge, and she liked the idea.

I love the way the kitchen smells when we make cookies. They look so festive and colorful when they are sitting on the trays. We really enjoy the tradition Mother started with us years ago. We will make the sugar cookies, decorated cutouts, chocolate chip, and an apple crunch with nuts. Sarah and Mother will make the apple crunch and cutouts; Ava, the chocolate chip; Gabby and Sophia will make the sugar cookies.

I prepare all the work stations with all the wet and dry ingredients everyone needs as well as setting out bowls, spoons, spatulas, whisks. I measure the ingredients, and I clean up to stay ahead of all the mess. I preheat ovens and take things in and out of the ovens. Then Sarah and all of us will decorate the cut-out cookies. That's when the fun begins. I will make all the different color frosting. This is our cookie system, which takes us a good eight hours, if not more, to get done.

Our girl family time! This is another one of the many Sawyer family traditions. We make many pots of coffee during the cookie making, not to mention Father and the boys will be out in the kitchen to be in our way and test the cookies as they come out of the ovens.

As I look around the room, I see a lot of yawning going on. The boys get up one at a time saying good night, and they will see us in the morning. Joshua says he is glad he doesn't have to sleep out in the field tonight, although he enjoys sleeping under the stars—the peace and quiet—in sleeping bags with the stories around the fire and a tented roof strung between trees. Oh, to be a blade of grass to hear what they talk about while out with the cattle. I can only imagine. Everyone turns in for the night.

Bump in the Night

I have been so exhausted all day, and I fall asleep as soon as my head hits the pillow. I hear noise in my room. I awake and turn my bedside lamp on. It's Rachel and Jackson!

They both shush me as to not wake the house. I am so excited to see them. I am wide awake. "Did anyone know you were coming home tonight? Is there anything more you need to bring from your car?" I am trying to open my eyes. I am tired.

Jackson explains, "No, I will get the rest tomorrow after breakfast. We just would like to sleep. We have had a long drive from Manhattan."

As he yawns, Rachel yawns. "The drive was incredibly long. My legs are a little stiff even though we stopped many times to stretch and walk around. We just wanted to get here, so we had not stopped but one time in the past six hours."

I look at both of them puzzled and confused. "Why did you drive?" I have a lot of questions that need to be answered. All this secrecy drives a person crazy.

They want me to sleep, and they will explain tomorrow at breakfast.

I wake up to the smell of coffee, and I smell my mother's famous oatmeal, an apple-cinnamon-banana-nut oatmeal mixture she throws together when the holidays approach. I love lying in my bed, trying to figure out what Mother is making by the smells coming from the kitchen. Rachel and I used to do that when we were younger. That's right! Jackson and Rachel snuck in last night while everyone was sleeping. I almost forgot.

I quietly take a shower, get dressed, and I head to the kitchen to have myself a bowl of Mother's oatmeal. This dish is one of the family's many favorites. We are all in the living room, scattered from one end to the other, still in our pajamas. Father was up and out before anyone. Father says, "I fed all the animals and got the eggs. I was looking around to see who owns the Land Rover in the driveway. Does anyone know whose that is? Did anyone call the vet? Rebekah, is it Noah? Was he stopping by today? Will he be here for Thanksgiving? When will we meet him?"

I reply, "What? No, Noah is not coming for Thanksgiving! He has not called, which means he is busy with college. You will meet him soon enough."

Father explains, "Before Jackson and Rachel come, I need to condition the bridle I left on the tack table prior to our holiday ride."

I look at Father. "What?" I am the only one that knows. Let me sit and feel important for a few seconds before I drop the news. "Wait, you guys don't know? Oh, wow, you guys are not aware. They are already here!"

Everyone looks at me and is asking why I did not say anything. They all have questions. When did they get here? I thought they were on a flight for today? I sit eating my oatmeal because as you may have guessed, it is impossible to answer everyone at the same time. There are ten family members asking me questions, so I wait.

Mother takes my bowl from me as if I weren't listening. I look up and flash my eyes to my mother with a smile. "When you give me my bowl and you are done asking me questions I cannot answer, I will tell you what I do know." I take my bowl back from Mother, and I start to eat again. I confirm a few things to my family. "They came in early this morning."

Father is asking, "Is that their Land Rover parked outside?"

I explained, "All I know is they drove from Manhattan to the ranch. They did not tell me anything else. I do know they were exhausted and are still sleeping."

Ava swiftly states," Well, let's just hang out until they wake up."

Everyone is anxious to know why they came so early. I ask my family to move the conversation to the living room. "I will clean up the kitchen." I clean up the kitchen as this decision gets me out of the twenty questions about Rachel and Jackson.

I roll up on the sofa next to my father. I place my head on his shoulder. I figure I will know when they come downstairs because it is going to get loud. There is a soft chatter, some of my brothers on the floor all stretched out, the girls draped over the chairs with pillows and blankets, starting to slip into a sleep. I look around the living room to see everyone napping. It's so quiet. I close my eyes.

I hear the collies running on porch, the tapping of their nails on the wood. Father has let them out of the barn this morning when he was out; sounds as if they are walking in a circle, then finally, they all bunched up on the porch as their nails stop tapping around the same area. We keep the collies in the barn in the warm, although they do need to get out and run a little and do their thing. We let them out around the house during the day when they are not working. They will go with us on the ride tomorrow. They love to run and investigate the area while we ride.

It's been two hours; everyone is waking up from their naps. The girls agree that they sleep well when everyone is here in the main house. We hear the unlock noise of the Land Rover from the living room. The boys get to their feet and out across the veranda to the back of the Land Rover they go to grab the rest of Jackson and Rachel's things and carry them to the second floor, where they will be staying. The boys pass Jackson and Rachel as they are coming down the stairs. Jackson thanks the boys for their help.

Jackson anxiously addresses the family, "Good morning! I guess since our things are already unloaded and in our room, we have time to sit, talk, and have a little breakfast."

Rachel reaches out to Mother and gives her a hug. "It has been almost a year," Rachel states.

"What a drive," Jackson says.

My family asks, "Why did you drive?"

Jackson said, "Give us a minute to grab a coffee, then we will tell you all about our news!"

I sit next to Rachel, not wanting to miss a word. Mother has been busy making breakfast for the second time today. Jackson and Rachel look at each other, all excited, and smile. Everyone is sitting in the kitchen, waiting for what Jackson and Rachel have to say.

Jackson tells everyone they sold their penthouse in Manhattan. "We will be flying back to pack it up, sign papers, and Rachel has to do some legal papers at the lawyers for her clothing line, then we will be back to the ranch to stay. The Land Rover is ours. We bought it after Rachel got her promotion. Rachel is able to work from home. She is no longer going to be traveling."

Rachel chimes in to say, "I will be managing fashion accounts across the United States as well as international accounts. I am no longer allowed to travel. Doctor notified me I am too stressed. I need to stay home. No more flying out."

Mother breaks in and asks, "Doctor said? What is wrong? Are you going to be okay?" Mother is up and working her way toward Rachel. Mother reaches Rachel and is hugging her. "Don't you feel good? What is happening?"

Rachel hugs Mother and continues to tell everyone, "I was offered this position a few years back and would not take it. I wanted to stay busy. I wanted to see the world, be successful, make a name for myself in the industry. I have extensive knowledge, demonstrated my ambition, and proved myself with my good work ethic. I have worked hard for the respect and trust of the industry. Now is my chance to take on more."

Mother says, "Are you overworked?"

Rachel says, "Oh, no, Mother. I am fine."

As Rachel embraces Mother, Rachel continues, "This is a wonderful opportunity for me. This time, I have taken the promotion when I was asked, and here we are!" Rachel says this with a smile as Jackson and Joe deliver even more news.

Joe and Sarah join them. "We"—Jackson points to all four of them—"have exciting news!"

"We are having a baby!" Jackson and Joe blurt out.

Our family is so excited. The holidays are going to be so busy with two new additions to the Sawyer family. Father asks, "There is only one? With this family's track record of having multiple births, but I guess it would be impossible to have our children have multiple births?"

Joe and Jackson look at each other and say, "Um, not sure. We will worry about that later."

Joe says, "I only found out early this morning."

The girls are only two months along. Rachel and Sarah shared their news together first. Jackson added, "I have been working remotely the past four years, hoping Rachel would have taken the opportunity earlier when it arose, but she told me the timing was not right. We said goodbye to our friends to start our chapter of our new life here, home with our family."

Jackson and Rachel say they need to speak to Father about just a small piece of land to build a house. Father looks at the boys. They all smile, look to Father then to Rachel and Jackson, and ask, "Where would you want to build?"

Father said, "We can ride the horses out and look tomorrow."

Rachel says, "We don't want to be too far away from the main house."

Both girls smile the biggest smile and say how fortunate they are to have such a loving family with so much approval and support. Mother, sitting next to Father on the sofa, tells everyone, "We were blessed years ago with healthy children, the ability to afford and run a cattle ranch. We have had many tests of strength along life's way, but the good Lord always came through. We needed the guidance to handle all of you and your endeavors as you grew up. I am so excited about grandchildren!"

We just toasted to the great news, and a knock came to the door. It is the Pizza Stone delivery person with five large pizzas, a super-three-foot turkey sub with all the fixings with a large cheese steak stromboli and salad; you would think we were feeding a small nation.

In all this excitement, we did not realize it was so late in the afternoon. Rachel says she could eat a grizzly bear. My brothers are grabbing the food to place it in the preheated low-temp oven to keep warm as Joe is paying the delivery man. The discussion of the ride starts. My brothers said, "Rachel and Sarah should not ride on horseback. It is too much bouncing since they are carrying our nieces."

I jump in, "Or nephews!"

Rachel and Sarah smile.

I said, "We will hitch the wagon to Duchess tomorrow for the ride since the new mothers should not be riding on horseback."

Mother and Father looked at the rest of the family and asked if there was anyone else holding out on them. We laugh, and some start with a line of a fib, only to see Mother give them the don't-you-even...look. She then says, "Only good, happy news, although your father and I will help you deal with whatever comes your way!"

I then proceeded to say, "I knew Sarah was holding out! She was bouncing around this house like a beach ball in a windstorm—"

Joe excitedly interrupts, "I just found out this morning. I am ecstatically happy. I have questions of when she found out. Sarah is good at secrets. I did not suspect a thing."

Our parents agreed this holiday will be one to remember, and the holidays ahead will hold just as many memories and excitement if not more.

COOKIES

We get a late start baking our cookies. I have all the different cookie stations ready. Everyone is busy mixing their ingredients. I am washing and running things all over the kitchen, making sure the areas are clean at all times and everyone has what they need.

Mother and Sarah are trying a sandwich cookie with fruit filling. Sarah is piping the filling in while the cookies are fresh out of the oven, letting the stuffed cookies cool a little on the sheet before I place them on the cooling racks. Mother says this type of cookie needs to be heated a little before serving, then it can be served with a scoop of vanilla ice cream.

The guys hear ice cream, and Father is the first to the kitchen, with the boys following close behind. All the girls are yelling, "Get out of the kitchen! You are in our way. No snitching cookies!"

"The cookies are too hot right now to eat," Mother says, "and the other cookies are raw, waiting to go in the oven. Don't eat raw cookies, Jacob! Jeremiah, what do you think you are doing? Joe, please get these boys back in the living room!"

Gabby tells the guys they will get a sample tray of cookies when we are done. Ava asks if there isn't anything they could be doing in the living room, maybe Christmas shopping for us since it is less than a month away. She doubts anyone has anything for anyone of us. Father gets them all together to go back to the living room.

Now the kitchen is ours again. "We have enough going on in this kitchen that we don't need men under our feet," Sophia claims. "If they come in the kitchen again, we will put them to work!"

Mother laughs. "They will stay out of our way for sure."

Sarah and Gabby start talking about Christmas and what they would like. Mother is wondering if the guys are listening. Gabby says, "Jacob and I will have everything we need once I start managing the Grilling Post, and two paychecks will be better than one to pay bills."

Sarah says she has everything she needs, with the baby coming. She told us she cannot wait until she can find out more about the little person she is going to have. Rachel agrees and mentions the summer house as a Christmas wish she has. Rachel has not mentioned this to Jackson or anyone. We look at her, puzzled. Rachel then looks to Mother and states she would like to redo the summer house. She is talking about requesting the summer house on the ride tomorrow.

Not sure what Jackson and Father will say, but that is what she wants for Christmas, to remodel the summer house and possibly add on to live right off the main house. Ava can't wait until her license for architecture comes in the mail. Joshua and she will be working out of their home office. They have their business cards and résumés out there in the architectural business world. They have had a few inquiries from companies to design things; they just need to send their credentials to the businesses that are interested. Then they will be busy. The prospective businesses will send information so Ava and Joshua can work off the information to design whatever is requested.

My sisters are asking me what I want for Christmas and if Noah is coming for Thanksgiving. I told them, "I am not sure, he was busy taking finals and told me he would contact me later on. I did not want to disturb him if he was testing or studying." I told them, "He will call. I don't know what I want for Christmas, I have everything I need." I smile as I am washing up the rest of the dishes. I add, "I am almost done with my college courses. I am a part of the most amazing family ever, and now I am going to be an aunt. What more could one person want?"

Sophia says, "A steady boyfriend."

I throw the tea towel at her and give her the evil eyes with a smile as I whisper, "Stop."

The girls are talking softer as to not arouse their husbands' suspicions. They are talking Christmas gifts, what they purchased, and how they will wrap it once it gets here. They sent the gifts to our parents' address in Mother and Father's name, so the guys won't know what they are getting, and they will not snoop.

That is silly, a grown man snooping. I know my brothers were good snoopers when we were kids. They would shake it, lift it, and guess, then open it to see what it was. Then they would have to retape what they unwrapped. Those boys were very good at opening gifts where they were taped. I remember one Christmas, our parents caught them and punished them by not giving them the gifts they bought them but gave clothes instead. They were really surprised when they did not get what they knew was for them. My parents would hide the gifts in the attic of the summer house. When my brothers found the gifts, they had already known Santa was a myth. They had been checking the gifts for three years before my parents caught them. The look on their faces was priceless. My parents have pictures of the boys that Christmas. The boys call those pictures their parole pictures.

All the girls were giggling. Rachel backed me up on that. I guess this year my sisters-in-law were entertained by an insider story about their husbands. They talked about this all through the cookie baking. Said they would have to keep an eye on them the little sneaks that they are.

Our cookies are done. Sample plates are made. My father and brothers are yelling to make sure we don't forget the scoop of ice cream that goes with that fruit-stuffed cookie. Gabby is working on getting them their scoop of ice cream. Mother tells them, "Be still for a moment."

After Mother warms the fruit cookie, the ice cream is placed on the plate. I told mother, "The fruit cookie looks fancy."

Gabby agrees and winks as she tells Mother, "That could be a new special dessert for Thursday nights at the Grilling Post."

Mother says, "If you would like to try it, we can do that." She smiles at Gabby.

Mother takes the plates in on a tray and hands them out to Father and my brothers. Jackson is saying how good the new cookie with ice cream is as others compliment, "The cookie tastes phenomenal."

Mother says, "We made more than enough for us and the luncheon at the church Sunday."

Sophia and Ava are arranging them on holiday festive trays for the church. Gabby puts wrap over them. Rachel places the trays on the far end of the counter until Saturday night. Sarah and I have finished cleaning the dishes. We wipe the counters off and clean the sinks. I throw all the linens we used in the washer. We are finally done. It's late and time for bed.

THANKSGIVING RIDE

*I*t's Thanksgiving Day. I hear Mother in the kitchen, opening and closing oven doors. I come down to the kitchen to help her. She just came from the walk-in cooler with the turkey. She is putting the turkey in the upper wall oven, and the ham is already in the lower wall oven. She tells me to set the timers on the wall ovens to start at 6:00 a.m. for the turkey; 9:00 a.m. start on the ham. End time on both: 3:30 p.m. I set the timers, and she hands me the potato filling and the garlic sour cream mashed potato casserole to place in the oven under the stove.

I set this timer to start at 1:00 p.m., setting the temperature a little lower than the normal until 2:00 p.m. I set the second phase to rise to normal temperature to complete the baking process and end at 3:30 p.m. I place the veggies in the four-tier crocks that are on the serving counter in the dining room. I add a little butter, salt, pepper, a dash of sugar and

94

turn them on. Mother has me place the sweet potatoes with marshmallows in the counter oven. I set the timer, and Mother and I go back to our rooms to get ready for the ride.

I look out the kitchen window and see Jacob, Jeremiah, and Joe hooking Duchess up to the wagon. The day is full of sunshine. There is a sparkle levitating in the air above the meadow. It looks like pixie dust because of the moisture in the air coming from Meadow Lake. It would have been a nice ride earlier this morning; there is more than likely a rainbow over the lake because of the sun's rays on the moisture in the air. Our ranch is named after this magical place: Shimmering Meadow Ranch. Our parents told us the story of when they bought the ranch, their friends asked what their one-hundred-thousand-acre ranch would be known as; at the time, they were not sure.

After they explored the property, they realized the pixie-dust-like shimmer above the lake in the meadow, which only happens when the air and temperature are perfect to make the air above the lake shimmer and sparkle like pixie dust, they realized what the name of the ranch should be. That is how our ranch got the name Shimmering Meadow.

I wait my turn to get into the bathroom. I lay on my bed, talking to Rachel. Rachel yells to Jackson, who is finishing up in the bathroom to let her some hot water. I ask Rachel, "Have you got a name picked out?"

Rachel replies, "No, not yet. Jackson and I agreed to wait at least five months to do anything about the baby. I also spoke to Sarah about this when she called to share her news, telling us she was going to let everyone know about her pregnancy when we were all together for Thanksgiving. Sarah and I were tossing around a few names, but we think waiting at least five months is being reasonable. Jackson and I discussed we do not want names that start with a J. Our family has enough of Js."

Rachel went on to say, "Jackson's parents are going to be excited. Jackson and I will stop by with his parents for an hour, not too long because I get so tired. Appearance is everything with his family, especially since they have a dinner party between Thanksgiving and Christmas for business associates of his father and mother. We need to tell his family, and Jackson said this would be the perfect opportunity since they will have friends over, and they can share the news as new grandparents."

We hear the shower has turned off. Jackson comes out of the bathroom fully dressed and ready to ride. I ask Rachel if I can get in the bathroom. I need to brush my teeth. She tells me to go right ahead as she needs to find her deodorant and hair ties. After I brush my teeth, I return to my room.

Jackson has gone downstairs to see if Mother needs help with the hot drinks and the cooler. I get dressed in warm clothes and wait for Rachel. We both walk the stairs to the kitchen and grab a piece of warm toast with Mother's homemade strawberry preserve.

We head to the barn. I jump on the wagon to help load the cooler of hot drinks. The boys are almost done saddling up their horses. They just need to make sure the cinch is tight. My brothers recheck the cinch on all the horses, and we are ready.

Everyone gets on their horse. Father tells us the horses are a little spunky but not too cantankerous today and to be careful; it is because of the snap of chilliness in the air that winds the horses up a bit. To me, it is not an irritable disposition. They just want to let loose a little; nothing wrong with that, although running is out of the question today. There is a chance of scattered snow flurries and possibly ice spots on the ground. When we get back, the boys will walk them and put them in the pasture to walk around a little until after Thanksgiving dinner then put them back in their stalls.

Sarah and Rachel are helped by Joe and Jackson to get on the wagon. Joe asks if they will be okay to handle the wagon with Duchess. The girls say, "We are pregnant. That does not affect our ability to think and react. Thank you," as they take the reins from Jackson.

Joe tells Jackson, "Pregnancy is going to be so much fun."

Jackson agrees as he mounts his horse and heads out to walk next to Joe.

Father leads us into the meadow and around the first ridge of the mountain. The mountain ridge is usually with at least four inches of snow by now. Not today. Definitely not cold enough, although it is chilly, and there are some areas with snow scattered on the ground.

Father is taking us to the ridge to ask Jackson if he sees a good spot to build. This area is only thirty minutes from the main house by horseback. There are a lot of tall ponderosa pines throughout our ranch, also beautiful blanket flowers on the forest floor with green moss like a thick carpet, Flodman's thistle, and cut-leaved coneflower cascading down the side of the ridge to the blue lake below in the spring and summer months.

The lake is so clear. You can see the reflection of the sky and mountain in the lake. It is just breathtaking with all that is around it. Father is asking if this spot is the perfect area for Rachel's house. Father stops the ride multiple times so Jackson and Rachel can see the area from different locations.

Talking to Jackson, Father asks, "What do you think of this area? There are many others not on a ridge that you can pick from. I just wondered if you would want this area since it is a great view within all this earthly beauty?"

Jackson anxiously tells Father he would like to ask Rachel about what she thinks of this area, and they ride to the back of the group to the wagon to speak to Rachel.

Jackson waits for Rachel to finish speaking to Sarah and asks, "Rachel, your father has asked me if we like this area to build our home. Is there a special place you would like? I am sure over the many years, as a young girl riding your horse the entire one hundred thousand acres, you had to have some favorite place. Is there any place special, any possibilities?"

Rachel says, "This is a perfect place, but I was thinking a little lower in elevation."

I smile at Rachel. Rachel says, "This is a special place. Mother used to ride with Rebekah and I, and we would sit, have a snack or lunch. Mother would let us play at times, take a nap, then ride to the water to splash around. As we got older, Mother taught us how to swim in this lake. I would like to keep this area as it is so we all may share the magic with our children as we raise them."

I ride up to Rachel and reach over to her, as I am on my horse, and hug her. No one knows, but this is where I would ride Dapple while Rachel was away at college. This is where I would come to feel like Rachel was with me.

Duchess is doing a great job with a smooth pull on the wagon. Sarah is holding the reigns. Rachel is yapping about baby things. Jackson is talking to the boys about the type of house they want, and Ava is hanging on every detail of the type of home Jackson wants for Rachel.

It is nice to be out with the family to get some fresh air along with the collies running all around. It makes for a wonderful day.

I ask Gabby, Ava, and Sophia to help me exercise the horses this week. We can get the horses exercised quicker if all of us participate. Sixteen horses and four of us should have this taken care of in no time. The guys chime in and let us know they will go along for a ride. It will be fun hanging out together, riding every other day. It won't seem like work at all. Our meals for the week will be easy fixes since we will have all those leftovers. We can help ourselves, and Mother won't have to do a thing.

Our ride is brisk and fresh. I love riding in the fall and winter; the weather is so revitalizing. The weatherman did say snow is coming. Father said, "It may be a big wintery mix of a storm later this week."

I hear Mother again telling Father we need to head back soon. It is chilly, and our Thanksgiving dinner will soon be ready. We have actually been out a lot longer than we anticipated. Believe it or not, four hours have passed since we started the ride.

We are drinking the coffee and hot chocolate we brought as Father is asking Jackson if Rachel has an idea of where she would like to build their home. Jackson says, "She wants to live closer, not so far out away from the main house."

Father says, "We will work our way back and chat about it over dinner."

I hear Sarah talking in the back of the group to Gabby about names. Sophia is asking the mothers about a themed nursery, cradle or crib, a crib that goes to four stages of a child's life. I am guessing Rachel has no idea about the four-stage crib Jackson has ordered to be delivered to the ranch.

Father leads us to the opposite direction from where we were about thirty minutes ago, asking

Jackson if they would like to build by the meandering creek or the lake by the meadow where we came from down on the flat of course. Rachel interrupted Father, asking if they can remodel the old summer kitchen that is attached to the farmhouse. We were wondering when she was going to ask. She spoke about it last night while making cookies. Father says, "Do you seriously want to be that close?"

Rachel replies, "We don't want to be so far out. We want to be close. We lived so far away for too long."

Ava says, "I want to sit with Jackson and Rachel during dinner to dicuss the remodeling of their new home. Could we do that?"

Rachel loves that idea and adds, "Since Jackson is letting it up to me, I am going to run with it. I have a few different floor plans I would like to put together. Do you and Joshua think you could combine what I like about the four floor plans I have then put it all together?"

Ava looks at Joshua then says, "Yes, no worries. We got this. This is going to be perfect." Ava tells Rachel she will work on this after dinner tonight.

Rachel is excited. As soon as we reach the barn, Rachel goes to the room, grabs the floor plans, and hands them to Joshua and Ava.

THANKSGIVING DINNER

The girls start pulling the food from the ovens. The guys are arranging the hot foods on the serving counter. Father and Jacob start carving the turkey. Joe and Joshua are slicing the ham. Jeremiah is stirring the sides while on the hot plates with serving ware.

We all stand around the table while Mother places the tray of glasses filled with ice-cold water, tea, and lemonade on the end of the serving counter, where everyone will take their drink before sitting at the table. Mother joins us around the dinner table as Father says, "All hold hands."

We bow our heads. Father starts the prayer: "Dear, Lord, we have a lot to be thankful for. Thank you for the food and bless the hands that have made the food. Thank you for life, health, and strength you have given us. We thank you for the news that our daughters and this family will be blessed with children a few months from now. I pray my family is blessed with the knowledge they need to live their lives healthy and happy. I am thankful every holiday and special occasion, for every day in between that brings our family together. God bless my family. I ask you in Jesus' name."

Everyone says, "Amen," with Father.

We are off to the serving counter, working our way down through the delicious food and making our way back to the table as we wait for everyone to be seated at their place. Father and Mother sit at opposite ends of the table, the girls to the right of Father, the guys to the left of Father, each one of my brothers and sister sitting across from their spouses on the other side of the table.

After the first couple of forks of food, Mother receives compliments, and the conversations begin. From Ava and Joshua's sketching Rachel and Jackson's floor plans for their house to Sarah and Joe talking about their baby, the plans for Christmas and every day in between, our house at the holidays is like a busy dining room in a restaurant. I look to both ends, where I see Mother and Father with the biggest smiles on their faces just listening to our holiday dinner conversation. I bet they are thinking back to how the holiday dinners have changed over the years since we have all grown up. The things that happened at this dinner table when we were kids to our dinner today. Important decisions were made here when we were growing up, our worlds' problems were solved here. The conversations ranged from Jeremiah's getting a D on his report card to a boy who cut Rachel's hair in school, high school detention for Jacob, Joshua's dating conversations with Jacob's first and last time smoking, and so much more. How the topics have changed since we were kids.

Ava and Joshua are at the end of the table, speaking softly in regard to what Rachel is looking for in her multiple designs of floor plans. Joshua shuffles through the small stack, flipping back and forth to see about support walls. What will be needed to get her floor plans to the summer kitchen to match up with all the floor plans and to make something amazing for Rachel and Jackson. Joshua says to Ava, "We will draw up some ideas tonight and check on changes they may have tomorrow. We need to get this project going. Ava, let us take a look at the inside of the summer kitchen after we are done eating with the family, then make a quick sketch of what we have to work with to see what we need to add as support walls or to fix some underlying issues with the foundation."

Father excuses himself from the dinner table and follows Ava and Joshua to the summer kitchen. Joshua looks at Father. "Wow, it is clean and empty."

Father states a fact: "You know your mother won't have dirt, webs, or any kind of filth whether the area is being used or not."

The three laugh. Joshua goes to the basement of the summer kitchen. Joshua notices this is superclean as well. Joshua takes Father and Ava to the basement of the summer kitchen to look at the walls and structure. "I think we are good with the structure. This is a nice area. We can offer to finish the basement and see what Rachel and Jackson would like to do with it. I don't know what they would have in mind. I thought Jackson mentioned a door so one can get out from the basement. I will ask what type of door, possibly a Bilco door. I will make a note to put that between the farmhouse and the summer kitchen just temporarily in our sketches before we do the completed drawing of the place. I will also put a glass French door to the back, looking out across to the mountain."

Ava adds, "I wonder if it is okay to add on to the summer house."

Father quickly states, "Most definitely. This summer kitchen is so tiny for a single family home. Add on wherever needed to make them comfortable." Father leaves Ava and Joshua to continue doing what they do best: make decisions and doodle, as Father puts it. Father comes back to the dinner table.

Jackson and Rachel excuse themselves from the table to make their way to the summer kitchen. Jackson is amazed at how clean the summer kitchen is, and Rachel begins to tell him how mother loves to clean. Ava and Joshua hear them coming down the stairs to the basement. Jackson says, "Oh, wow, we are going to like the office down here. It is the perfect space for us."

Jackson looks at Rachel. "I was thinking we could share space, right?"

Rachel begins her thoughts out loud on the basement. "I would like soundproof cubicles to work from so I can tack notes around my desk, and I would not need anything on the walls. Also, with Jackson and I sharing space, the cubicles will be a sound barrier for when we are on the phone."

Jackson says, "That's perfect! We will order two."

Ava and Joshua smile and say, "We can get that built right into the opposite sides of the room if both of you are okay with that. It will probably save you money."

Ava will check on that. Rachel actually wants the desks facing each other with the cubicles around and between each other in the center of the room. Rachel goes on to say, "If they are facing each other, the sound will absorb around them and not escape to interrupt the other person across the room, which, in this case, is Jackson." She smiles with a little laugh.

Ava then says, "Done!"

Jackson asks Joshua and Ava if they can place the door to the front of the summer kitchen basement and use the largest thick glass French doors they can order, the ones with blinds in so they do not need any frilly window treatments. Rachel states the fact that this side of the house gets the wind, and they would like a thick safety glass in case something blows into the window, it should withstand the impact. Joshua makes a note about the need for thick safety glass. "We will check on that as well," Joshua says. "I would like both sides of the door to open with a screen to bring the fresh air into the office in the spring, summer, and early fall months."

Ava says, "No problem. Noted."

Rachel says, "Let's get back to the family. I will help clean up so we can start the Christmas decorations. Mother was talking about doing them early so we could spend more time together."

As Rachel, Jackson, Ava, and Joshua arrive in the dining room, they hear a ruckus in the living room. The dining room is all cleaned up. The dishwasher is running. The guys and Father are getting the boxes together for the outside of the farmhouse. Joshua, Jacob, and Joe go to the second floor veranda to drape the prelit pine garland to the railing. Mother reminds them to start in the back corner and work their way around to the front corner to plug the garland in, and the same goes for the first-floor prelit garland on that railing, making sure they match. Jackson and Jeremiah tell Mother, "We got this."

Father just put the ten-foot tree by the fireplace. Sophia, Gabby, and Sarah start to shape the tree. Gabby is on the ladder, shaping the top, working her way down to Sophia, who is shaping the middle, and Sarah is working around the bottom. Gabby said she is glad the tree is prelit. The girls agree. They enjoy the time spent together placing the ornaments on the tree. Mother and I work our way to the storage boxes that were left in the middle of the living room floor. We take out the large wreath and place it on the hook above the fireplace on the dining room side. Mother arranges the nativity scene on the mantel in the living room; I place the realistic-looking green pine garland with twinkle lights along the underside of the mantel on the hooks provided by Father, which makes it easy to hang.

Mother compliments the girls on the swell job of placing the bright-red balls with gold designs on the tree. Sarah grabs the tree skirt of red and gold, gets down on the floor, and crawls underneath, arranging the skirt with no wrinkles. Father always does the garland on the Christmas tree. He will do that when he finishes up with the boys, then our tree is complete and will look beautiful.

We put the Christmas gifts under the tree, along with the stocking stuffers in the stockings on Christmas Eve. Our parents have always done it this way to make it look as though Santa was doing his job. This tradition never changed. The house is decorated for Christmas. Sophia makes hot chocolate for everyone and brings it to the living room for us to relax and enjoy.

HOME FOR THE HOLIDAYS

*T*he next four days we lounge around the house just catching up. We want to know what everyone has been doing. We talk about friends we have not seen in a long time and just whatever comes to mind. The family is having such a great time being together hours are passing like seconds.

Sarah has been showing Father and Joe the finished website for the ranch. It is perfect! The website should attract a lot of new cattle buyers. They are discussing when the site should go live; they are deciding Christmas or New Year's Eve. I hear the anxiousness in Sarah's voice as she shouts, "Christmas! I think Christmas is too early. Let's set the site live on New Year's Eve midnight."

Joe looks to Father as Father decides, "New Year's Eve at midnight is a great time."

Sarah eagerly says, "I have another surprise about the site." She continues to elaborate by stating she has some glitz she threw into the ranch name as it comes up on the screen because, after all, the ranch is known as Shimmering Meadow. With that said, Sarah reaches over Joe, typing the ranch name in the title bar at the top of the screen, then presses enter. The ranch logo comes up along with the Sawyer name, which takes up the entire screen. Sarah then moves the arrow to the logo and does a right click with the mouse. There are little bits of shimmer within the site as all the information comes to life on the screen.

Father smiles. "Nice touch, Sarah."

Joe adds, "She had a lot more, and I told her we needed to tone it down a bit."

Father agreed it is just enough to make it stand out from other cattle sites.

Ava and Joshua are doodling to get the highlights from the specifics of the floor plans on the papers into the summer house. They are working from the bottom up and are talking to Jackson and Rachel. They will notify them when the first draft is done to review. Rachel is getting excited, knowing they will review the first draft in two days.

Mother is looking at her new cookbook for a possible dish to impress the family at Christmas dinner. She is asking Sarah what new dish she will bring to the table this Christmas. Gabby has a recipe of homemade braided bread with cranberries she would like to try with a drizzle of vanilla cream cheese frosting on top. Mother and Sarah like the sound of that.

Father is back on the recliner, reading his evening paper, every now and then looking over his glasses to see what is happening in the room. He puts his paper down and sips his hot chocolate and asks Jeremiah if Sophia and he are opening a private practice or going to join a practice when he is done with his residency. Father says, "Six years are going to fly by in no time."

Sophia tells Father they are not sure, although they are leaning more toward a private practice when they return in six years.

Father says, "I know Jeremiah wanted to do house calls that would be nice and convenient for patients who cannot drive nor have transportation. It would be a great idea. Not sure how much insurance you would need, but check into the house calls. No one does that anymore. I wish our family doc had the time to come to the house."

Sophia says, "We will be working out all the details over the next six years while Jeremiah is in his residency. There is so much to think about. Financially, we are looking at the cost of renting with utilities, trash, insurance versus a private practice with the same expenses. The only difference is we realize if we own, it is ours after a few years. We will let you know what we decide when we get back.

"We wanted to corner Jackson on some numbers. Figured Jackson would know how to get numbers closer to what we need in order to check the difference. Also, Jackson may uncover some things we never thought of."

Jackson stated, "That won't be a problem I can get on that after the holidays, not that you would need the information that soon, but I could get you roundabout figures. Numbers will definitely change in six years. I could probably help you check into the insurance part for house calls. It is possible you may have to jump through hoops and you want this in place before you start your practice. Let me speak to a few of my friends who take care of insurances."

Jeremiah says, "I only ask you because I remember you dabbled a little in the real estate business selling and buying properties before you got into the Wall Street numbers game. Thank you for checking things out for us. Insurance is a little tricky to sometimes understand."

Jackson reassures Jeremiah, "I will get it all figured out for you so you at least have an idea what you would be looking at when your residency is over in six years."

Ava asks the guys to run outside to gather wood for the fireplace so when we come home from dropping the cookies, the fire will still be going. Father says, "No worries. Looks like it may be a late night at the fire. We will all be here when everyone gets back."

Father is looking through his desk drawer for information on the new cattle pick up this coming spring. Our farmhouse feels even cozier this holiday because of Jackson and Rachel's not having to leave. It is so nice to have everyone home. Looks like I get my roommate back plus one and a half.

Rachel and Jackson are announcing they have to make an appearance for a couple of hours at his parents' house, then they will be back. Jackson warms up the Land Rover, and in fifteen minutes, they are walking out the door and on their way.

Mother says, "Hey, girls, time to take the cookies to the church." Mother grabs two trays. Sophia, Gabby, Ava, and I pick up two trays as well. The covered trays of cookies are placed in the back of the Suburban floor. There are two trays that don't fit. Ava and Gabby sit in the back seat with Sarah. Mother and I are in the front. I start the Suburban and drive to the church. We are discussing how we don't like it being dark so early in the evening. I tell everyone, "It makes me tired, and I think it is later than it really is."

In about thirty minutes, we are at the church. We grab our trays of cookies and head for the double red doors. We are greeted by Sophia and Mother's friend Leona, who has been a member of the church since she was a little girl. Leona's mother and my grandmother Bertha were good friends. Leona leads us to the church hall, and we place the cookies on the dessert table for tomorrow's luncheon. Mother asks Leona if she thinks pies and cakes would be okay for Christmas, and Leona responds, "Pies and cakes would be just fine. Thank you."

Mother tells Leona we have to get back to the house, that we have plans for tonight, and we will see everyone at church tomorrow. We all say goodbye, and we are on our way to the ranch, chatting about church tomorrow.

We arrive, and as we make our way to the living room, we notice Rachel and Jackson are home from his parents, and Sarah is napping on Joe. Father calls Mother to the large two-person recliner in the room as he throws a blanket on them from the back of the recliner. I grab a pillow and blanket to lie on the floor in front of Jeremiah and Sophia. Everyone is all snuggled up with their significant other. I get up, check the doors to make sure they are locked. I head back through the kitchen, and I cannot believe who is standing in our living room. It's Noah. I run across the room and hug him. I am glad he is here. I ask if he has met everyone as I lock the door behind him.

Noah says, "I met your brothers and father. I already know your mother from riding this past summer. I have not met any of your sisters."

I start to introduce my sisters-in-law when I get to my sister. Noah's mouth drops. "No way," he says.

"What?" I reply.

"You are identical? You never told me," he says.

"I thought I would tell you when the time was right," I said.

"You have triplets for brothers," Noah said.

"Except for Joe," I chimed in.

My family is laughing hysterically. They are asking why I did not tell him we were multiple and identical.

I tell my family, "It just never came up. I did not think we would be so involved. After all, we just met, and we rode horse together. It never crossed my mind to tell Noah."

"Poor Noah is going to be so confused until he figures out who's who," implied Sarah.

"He will catch on after a few days," Father said.

I look at Noah and say, "You are staying?"

"Seriously, Rebekah, where else do I have to be?" Noah states.

"That's great! I mean, well, you know…I am glad you are here with us!" I tell him. "I will pull the rollaway bed out from under mine, and you can sleep there, if that is okay with you, Mother…Father?"

"The house is full, and we don't want him sleeping on the sofa. We trust you both will be aware of where you are and respect your parents as well," Mother states as she looks to Father, and my father nods his head yes with a smile.

"Where else would he sleep?" Joe said.

"Not with any of us. Our rooms are already full," everyone jokes and is laughing with Noah and me.

We go to my room on the second floor after stopping at his jeep to grab his things. He is telling me, "I spoke to your father and asked if I could stay for a few weeks, that I was between colleges actually, transferring to the college we visited in town."

I look at him and say with a big smile, "My father is going to let you live here until you start college with me in February?"

"Your father said it would be fine, although your father said after the holiday, everyone goes back to their home. I will be moving to the attic. I did speak to your father about doing chores and pay to stay here. I do not want to stay for nothing. I have my trust, and I can pay my way," Noah stated. "I am not here to take advantage of anyone. Your family is nice. I really enjoyed the time I had with them before you came back with the crew you were with." He laughs. "There is just so many in your family, and everyone looks like each other. I love it! Your family is amazing."

"I am glad you like my family. I am sure it was a little overwhelming at first when you came in, with all my brothers, my father. I did not really give you fair warning about the size of my family. just that I had brothers and sisters. I count my sisters-in-law as sisters," I say with a giggle.

"Yes, you do come from a large family. If Jackson survived, I can too," Noah stated.

"Noah, sounds like you are going to be here with me for a while," I say.

Noah looks my way and says, "Maybe."

Noah and I have his bed made, his things hung in the closet. I moved some things to other drawers so Noah can use the empty drawers. He is all settled in.

We work our way back downstairs to my brothers' bringing in firewood. Noah asks if he can help with anything. My brothers take him outside for more wood. My parents say, "He can stay in your room because I think we should move Rachel and Jackson to the attic for now until the summer kitchen is redone for them. Noah can sleep in Rachel's bed when they move to the attic."

I smile and say, "Okay, thanks. I have a roommate again."

We hear the guys on the porch. They are stomping the snow off their boots, sounding like a herd of elephants. The door to the living room opens; they are loud, laughing, talking having a great time. Noah is yapping and carrying on with them like he's known them for years. My brothers are telling me how they approve of Noah.

Father is putting more wood on the fire. He turns to the family and tells them, "Noah will be staying, and Noah is welcome to stay for as long as he wants."

My brothers are saying stupid, silly things, kidding around. Noah loves the harassing they are giving me. I look at my brothers, roll my eyes, and remind them we all sleep in the same house; at some point they do need to close their eyes. Now they get quiet.

They have had the wrath of Rebekah a while back and didn't think it was funny, although I did.

Noah is curious, asking my brothers what I did to them that make them afraid I could do something again. Joe started by saying his perfect shadow looked somewhat like he had a mange animal on his face, not attractive. "I had to shave," Joe says as Joshua, Jacob, and Jeremiah start laughing.

Jackson says, "Oh, Rebekah, you are good!"

Joshua then says, "She put fresh horse apples in Jacob and my boots one time. We had new stinky boots for a long time, nothing like the smell of new leather smelling like horse apples. Ugh yuck!"

Jeremiah said, "She rolled me in cow pies in my Sunday best. Watch out for her trickery."

Noah and Jackson are congratulating me for taking care of myself. I said, "Definitely! I am just a small girl in a family with a lot of brothers. I know how to handle them!"

My brothers are laughing. They all agreed I did well. It was not funny at the time, but they now admit it is funny looking back. Mother and Father were not impressed the Sunday Jeremiah got rolled in the cow patties. We were a little late for church. Mother and Father yawn, get up from their recliner, and fold the blanket as they say their good nights and head to bed.

Sophia, Ava, Gabby, Rachel, and I go to the kitchen to set the coffeepot to start at 4:00 a.m. for the guys. We place a stack of bowls, plates, and utensils in the dining room on the serving counter. We can hear my brothers and Jackson briefing Noah that the guys get up early to feed the animals. Noah says, "Well, I better turn in. I'm doing chores so I can stay. I want to pull my weight around here too, ya know."

Noah and I climb the flight of stairs to my bedroom on the second floor. I tell him, "You can sleep when you are done feeding the animals. My brothers feed the cattle and horses so Father can sleep in."

Noah said, "That's nice. Sounds like that is a good idea. I will take a shower when I am done helping."

I said, "Yes, you will need the shower."

I let him in the bathroom first, then it's my turn. I brush my teeth, comb my hair, get my PJs on. I get to my bed. I reach over to turn the light off, and he asks me what Christmas is like with my family. "Oh, I don't know. It's always been magical for us growing up. Our parents do the gift placing under the tree Christmas Eve, so my siblings and I always thought Santa was here. Our parents would put Christmas cookies with a glass of milk and carrots for the reindeer on a plate on the hearth of the fireplace. We were always told Santa likes a snack while he was on his long journey around the world, stopping at every house, placing gifts under the tree and in kids' stockings. It was fun when we were kids. I would say it is still fun even now that we are all grown up.

"Then there is Christmas dinner. We have surf and turf with all the sides. You will enjoy Christmas dinner. I am sorry you missed Thanksgiving. Were you planning on being here for Thanksgiving?"

Noah tells me, "I wanted to be here for dinner, but Fran asked me to stop over with her and the family. I could not very well say no, knowing all she did for me growing up. When I was seven, Fran took me to her house to live. Fran figured she could watch me there just as well as she could watch me at my aunt and uncle's house because Fran had a family too.

"I liked it at Fran's. She always treated me as one of her own. My uncle had the lawyer draw up papers so if anything would happen to him, Fran would get me and my trust to take care of me.

"Fran did help me a lot. I told everyone she was my mother. I did not think I needed to explain my life to anyone, except you and your family. Fran never used my money for me. She never touched the trust. Her husband always purchased things for me with their money without batting an eye."

Noah yawns, and I reach over to turn the light out. I hear Rachel and Jackson come up the stairs. She grabs their pillows and blanket. Jackson grabs the mattress and drags it to my side of the room. Rachel says, "It has been a while since we had a slumber party." I am looking at her and Jackson. I look doubtful and comment, "Really? I am exhausted."

Jackson and Rachel want to talk more to Noah. I know what they are doing. "I think it's great, you guys, but can't this talk session wait until tomorrow? You can get to know him when you are out at the barn feeding and bringing in the wood."

I yawn and reach for the light once more. Rachel says, "Yeah, what about me? I need to get to know him a little more. What if he thinks you're me?"

"Rachel, please!" I ask, "Can I get some sleep? All I want is sleep."

I fall asleep to Jackson and Rachel's yapping to Noah.

It is 2:00 a.m. I throw my legs over the side of my bed to run to the bathroom. I trip over Jackson and fall on the floor next to Rachel. "Oh my!" I say out loud. I forgot they were all on my side of the room. I get to my feet and head to the bathroom.

I hear everyone is up and talking again. I come from the bathroom and apologize to Noah. Noah says, "It's okay. Let them talk. I am not tired. I actually enjoy their company. I enjoy talking to your family. I need to know all I can about everyone, and I love to hear all the family stories."

"Okay," I say as I step over Rachel and Jackson to crawl back into my bed. "I am going back to sleep. Enjoy your visit. See everyone in the morning." I close my eyes, and I am sleeping.

I hear all these voices in my room. Did I fall asleep in the living room? I hear my other siblings as well, but it can't be. I roll over and see Noah finally sleeping. I close my eyes; I can hardly keep them open. Thank goodness he is getting sleep before having to help in the barn.

I hear the alarm go off; it's 4:00 a.m. The smell of coffee brewing in the kitchen made its way through the entire house. I hear a bunch of footsteps and voices in my room. Nah, I think I am probably dreaming.

The toilet flushes multiple times. I turn; Noah is gone. Jackson is gone. I see the bathroom light on; Jacob comes out of my bathroom. I sit up, stretch. I wipe my eyes, turn the lamp on, and as the light shines across my bed, I can see Ava, Sophia, and Gabby. I say, "Jeez, where are Joe and Sarah?"

Joshua confesses, "Don't be silly. Sarah is over on the recliner in the corner of your room, sleeping. Joe was up first and is waiting for us downstairs."

As I turn the lamp off, I put my head on the pillow. I ask, "How many nights will everyone be camping in my room?"

Gabby chimed in, "Everyone just wants to get to know Noah better. We have not had a slumber party in quite a while, we figure it's time." They are all telling me about how Noah is a great guy, and he is a good fit for the family. They were wondering what I think of Noah. "I must confess he is a dream. I love Noah," I eagerly let them know. "We have only been seeing each other for a year. We did a lot of riding this past year. He is easy to talk to, and I know a lot about him.

"I am actually glad he is here. He would make a great husband. just not sure if he would pick me. although I have to be honest. I fell in love with him the first time I saw him. He is perfect for me. Not sure if I am perfect for him. He did not have much of a family life growing up like us. We always had each other, and I really want him to be a part of our family, but we are not moving as fast as you did. You girls were engaged after one and a half years of dating. I don't even know if Noah is ready for that. Noah and I will be starting college in February."

The girls reassure me they see how he looks at me, and they think he feels the same.

Rachel, Ava, Sophia, and Gabby are scrambling between two bathrooms. While some are taking a shower, the others are brushing their teeth, applying a facial mask for twenty minutes; they peel their masks off, and we are spread throughout Rachel and my bedroom, doing our hair and makeup, getting dressed. By the time we are done, the guys are in from the barn, and it's their turn to hit the showers.

My sisters and I make our way downstairs to the kitchen. I was the last one in the line of all my sisters heading down the stairs when Noah was on his way up the stairs. He grabbed me, giving me a hug and a smooch as he passed, telling me, "I will see you downstairs after my shower." He gave me a wink and a smile.

"Okay, see you soon," I said with a smile.

All the girls gather around Father and Mother at the island in the kitchen. Father asks, "How did everyone sleep? I heard some rustling upstairs last night, some giggling and laughing. You did not hear it, Rebekah? You must have been sleeping soundly last night."

I told Father, "Yes, I was tired."

Ava asks, "What's that delicious smell?"

Mother tells her it is the breakfast casserole she has in the oven. She says, "It is a new recipe I found on the Internet and decided to try it."

We hear a ruckus upstairs. Father says, "Oh no." He looks at me and says, "Tonight sounds like it should be pretty interesting too."

I look at everyone and roll my eyes. Sophia says, "This guy is in love with you, Rebekah!"

Gabby, Sarah, and Rachel keep telling me they see the way he looks at me, how he says the things he says. Ava and Sophia agree. With a giggle and jokingly stern tone, I tell them, "Quit looking at my boyfriend!"

The guys are storming down the stairs like a herd of cattle. They are pushing and running through the kitchen, and Noah is right there with them. Noah breaks away from my brothers, approaches Rachel and me. He stands there looking at us because we both have bibs on with a long-sleeved button-down shirt. Jackson pours Rachel a coffee and tells Noah, "It won't be long and you will be able to tell them apart."

Jackson hands the coffee to Rachel. Noah says to Jackson, "I don't know. I hope I can figure this out soon. The holidays are going to be tough for me if I can't figure out the differences between them."

I reach out, and I am by his side. He swings me around, and I tell him, "You are the perfect fit with my brothers."

He says, "Perfect fit just with your brothers?"

I tell him, "You are a perfect fit for me too!" He smiles and hugs me tight.

Sophia asks, "What was the ruckus upstairs?"

The guys say, "Nothing, why?" as they bump Noah and pull him away from me, and to the living room they go.

Gabby then replies, "There was a lot of laughing, yelling, and loud noise coming from the second floor stairwell."

The guys again say nothing. I see Joe whisper to Sarah. Sarah smiles, shakes her head yes, and she looks my way. Sarah walks over to our parents and pulls them to the living room. I look around the corner of the far end of the fireplace from the dining room to see my parents huddled with Sarah. Sarah is talking a mile a minute to Mother and Father. Father has the biggest smile I have ever seen. As Father hugs my mother, he says, "I know all about it, her brothers and I were already notified. We are going to be busy the next few weeks."

I wonder what that is all about. Maybe a surprise homecoming for Jackson and Rachel? Maybe a baby shower for Rachel and Sarah, a party for Gabby possibly because of taking over the Grilling Post? It could be a birthday party for my brothers. Christmas present for the mothers-to-be? Hmm, any number of things. I am sure I will need to help do something. I won't feed anything into the whispering. I will just wait. I am sure I will find out eventually.

Sophia pulls the casserole out of the wall oven and places it on the serving counter atop the hot plate in the dining room. Everyone grabs a plate. Father tells us we need to get ready to head to church after we are done eating. Everyone goes to their rooms, gets changed, and we are off to church. Mother states, "We are not staying for the luncheon. I would like to get home to be with our family."

Father says, "It won't hurt a bit to stop in for a second."

Mother looks his way. "All right, but we will make it a quick visit then it's back to the ranch."

Father smiles and embraces Mother. "Now that Jackson's parents know about the baby, don't you want to tell your friends?"

Mother looks at Father and smiles. "Yes, I would like to share the good news with friends at church. I did not think of that."

The church service ends and Pastor Rob, in closing, invites everyone to come to the luncheon. We filter through the pew, and out into the aisle, we make the left to join the congregation in the church hall. Mother catches up to Leona to tell her about the babies that will be blessing our family in nine months or so. She goes on to share all the happenings of the family. Leona is hanging on every word, smiling, shaking her head in deep attention with what Mother is telling her. Sarah and Rachel stand by Mother's side as she is talking. Leona asking questions to the girls; the girls answer in short, abrupt comments because they have not settled on a name, and if they have, no one really knows. It is too soon.

Mother has a crowd around her as more women join the group. Sarah leaves the group to find Joe and the rest of the family. Sarah, Ava, Gabby, and Sophia see Noah speaking to the pastor for fifteen minutes if not more. They walk my way and ask how Noah knows the pastor. I say, "Gee, I don't know."

We watch as the pastor shakes his hand. We hear the pastor tell Noah, "You let me know, and I will get it scheduled. Glad to have you in our congregation. Will I see you next week?"

I hear Noah answer, "Yes, for sure. See you next Sunday!"

"I got this." I inform my sisters as I am walking toward Noah. I latch on to Noah's arm, asking him if he knows the pastor.

He says, "I just met him today. He is a nice pastor, not pushy at all about church."

Okay, so I left it at that and got in the jeep to go home.

We are back to the ranch, and everyone can't wait to get out of their Sunday best. Mother calls us to the kitchen. The counter has turkey sandwiches, a bag of pretzels with dip, a jar of pickles Mother canned this past summer with a salad and multiple dressings to choose from. As we made our way through the little lunch buffet, Mother hands us a glass of freshly made lemonade and a cupcake. Mother found a new recipe in her cookbook: cranberry cupcakes. Mother wants us to try them. Everyone loves them. Gabby is asking Mother if she can make those for the Grilling Post and fancy them up a bit.

Mother tells her, "Most definitely. I can put the crystalized sugar on top. That will spruce them up a bit to serve at the Grilling Post."

Gabby says, "Speaking of the Grilling Post, my parents want to retire early. They are asking me to stop by their lawyer's office to sign papers. They want me to take the Grilling Post over before the end of the year."

Jacob replies, "The lawyer's messenger dropped the papers by the ranch this morning. I put the papers upstairs on my dresser."

Gabby rolls her eyes and says, "Oh, I guess later I will read over the papers and get them signed. I just thought I was going to take over after the New Year. I don't know why they are being so pushy. I guess I should not say pushy. They are just in a rush for things to happen to retire so they may move to Arizona. You know they found a really nice home, with extra rooms for when Jacob and I come to visit. They are excited about moving on to do absolutely nothing but enjoy life."

Gabby mentions a going-away party and would like Sarah to get the ball rolling. Gabby wants to plan a party at the Grilling Post and suggests the party be planned on a Sunday after church since the Grilling Post is closed.

The girls sneak away to the living room. Ava grabs pens and paper. She returns to the large sofa where we are lounging to hear the thoughts for the going-away party for Gabby's parents. Ava hands us a pen and paper. Gabby starts talking about food for the menu she would like for the gathering. Sophia yells for mother to help with ideas, baked goods, and the cake of Gabby's choice. Sarah is taking notes as well. She has the layout form of the Grilling Post restaurant in front of her, making changes as to where the tables for guests will be placed and the dance floor. Gabby states, "I will need to make the chef aware of the date as well as the wait staff. We may only need four waitresses and four waiters. The kitchen staff will be the normal crew. I will call them later on today so they may place this day on their calendar."

Sophia is asking, "Which Sunday?" Sarah is asking for Gabby's parents' list of friends and other family so she can get the dining area complete with enough tables and chairs. She suggests that Gabby use linens, dishes, and glassware that are used for wedding receptions from the pavilion at the Grilling Post.

Gabby thinks that is a great idea. She wants this to be special. Sophia is suggesting beautiful tall full centerpieces with large flowers, sprigs of pussy willows and wisteria draping from the sides along with green ivy and baby's breath to set it off.

Sophia continues, "We can use the lace lavender overlays on the white linen tablecloths for the tables to set the centerpieces off and bring the tables together. They will look so perfect!" Sophia sits next to Sarah to jot her ideas down. Ava is asking about candles throughout the Grilling Post to set the mood of fine dining. Gabby agrees.

Mother is going through her cake recipes to find the perfect cake for this special occasion, possibly a pudding or a fruit-filled cake with a few layers surrounded by cupcakes. Mother would prefer a cream cheese, which is a normal sweet frosting. She searches the Internet and her cookbooks, looking to find something spectacular for this event. She then will get her ideas together and show Gabby.

The guys are saying they plan on going for a ride, so out to the barn they head, Noah right along with them. Sophia, Rachel, Ava, and Gabby are going on about the party for Gabby's parents. Mother and I are looking at the cakes she has narrowed down. Now to pick one of the five she has listed. I ask her if there should be three different kinds. "I was thinking two for the cupcakes and one for the cake. This will be my third time making a cake for an event this large. How many people will be attending?" Mother asks.

Gabby and Sophia are working on the list. They heard Mother ask, and Sophia has her hand up, asking Mother to wait. Gabby is making a list of all the friends her parents know, and Sophia is making a list of family. Gabby wants to keep it small but have a large impact on her parents. All kinds of ideas are being mentioned.

Gabby starts a fire in the fireplace and sits back on the sofa with her feet up. She mentions she is really cold. She hopes she is not getting sick. We are running out of things and ideas to donate to the thoughts of the party.

Mother mentions she is going for a nap, and then she will discuss her ideas about the grand dessert later. Mother always has fantastic ideas.

I am hopeful that tonight holds more sleep then last night, although trying to sleep last night was almost impossible. I am doubtful about tonight as well.

Sarah and Sophia say, "We got a good start on what we are doing for Gabby's parents' going-away/retirement party." Sarah and Sophia are yawning. Mother has moved into the recliner and is fast asleep.

I lay on the sofa, close my eyes, and in a bit, I am roasting. I must have pulled the cover on me from the back of the sofa. I kick the covers off, and I open my eyes, and I am lying on Noah's lap. The guys are back from their ride. Noah is running his fingers through my hair, letting my hair fall, twisting and flipping through his fingers. He does this continuously until my eyes are closed and I fall back to sleep.

I wake to the sound of the news on the television and the smell of stuffed shells with garlic bread, spaghetti with meatballs. Noah is sleeping, and I want to see if Mother needs help in the kitchen. I get out from under Noah's grasp and make my way to the kitchen. I wash my hands, set the table, and I am off to the living room to bring everyone to the table to eat. We all take a plate, go through the buffet line of food and to the table in the dining room for our family dinner. After dinner, we clean up and head to the living room. Father is adding wood to the fire.

The guys are talking about a movie we could gather around to watch. Father is surfing the channels, looking at the menu of upcoming movies for the night. The boys want a Western; the girls want a chick flick, so Father puts on an old Western that is both. Great pick! An O'Hara and Wayne movie, this one is my favorite.

An hour into the movie, I ask if anyone wants popcorn. I go to the kitchen to put the popcorn in the microwave. I'm in the kitchen after a few minutes Noah appears and offers to help. I tell him, "The popcorn industry needs to make large bags."

Noah laughs and makes small talk about my family. "Your family is nice. I feel lucky to be here. To have every one of your family members as a part of my life makes me feel comfortable and loved."

I tell him, "It can be a lot at times, but yeah, it's a wonderful feeling to be a part of this many people."

He says, "I really enjoy being at the ranch, your company, and I would like to know what your plans are after college classes are over."

I answer, "I am not sure. I was tossing a few things around, and I just don't know what I want to do. I do know I want to stay with my family. I could move away, but why when I can help out and do not have to commute to the ranch to help. So I was thinking of waiting to see what happens with my brothers and their career choices. If their careers take them away from the ranch, I will stay in their cabin on one of the far corners of the ranch, then I can do my job and help out on days I am not working. I am not sure, though. It is a wait-to-see kind of thing. Why?"

Noah says, "It's nice to know the plans of the person you want to spend time with, don't you think?" He smiles and tells me the microwave went off.

I asked him, "Speaking of time, how long were you here before I arrived Saturday night?"

"I arrived right after you left," he replied. "I was invited in by your brother Jacob. I met your father and the rest of your brothers. I must say, I did not realize your brothers were so identical, and Joe looks like one of the triplets. Of course, they resemble your father. I really had to pay attention. I watched you interact with all your brothers, and it is amazing how you can tell them apart, just amazing."

"You have to remember, I have lived with them all my life. I am knowledgeable of their personalities, mannerisms, and little quirks. Jeremiah is outgoing. Jacob is somewhat of a jokester, a little smart-ass. And Joshua is shy. They are all intelligent but very different in personalities. You will figure them out. What am I saying? You already have. They love you. All of you pal around like you have known each other for years, laughing, joking, those stupid wrestling moves they do. You fit in really well with my brothers."

Noah laughs. "Yes, I have noticed, but some qualities about them are similar. It will take me a little longer than an hour or so hanging out and a three-hour horse ride to get to know them, especially since three look exactly alike. I have not picked out each personality which makes them easier to tell apart."

"I am sorry I am so much work. I would not blame you if you threw in the towel and rode off into the sunset," I say this, knowing he won't of course. I know he likes a challenge.

I hand Noah three large bowls of popcorn on a large tray. He takes them to the living room, hands one to my parents, the other two between my siblings, and comes back into the kitchen. "You know, when your brothers are with their wives, it helps even more to tell who is who."

I agreed. "Yes, it helps me, too, at times." I begin to tell him, "They will start to dress a little different when they start their careers."

"Oh, I cannot wait to hear what careers they chose. I'm sure I won't believe it when you tell me," he says.

I start to tell him what each one has chosen to do with their life.

"Will Jacob and Ava still be living on the ranch?" he asks. "After all, a physicist is a lab rat kind of career."

I reply, "I am not sure. He wants to work remotely and fly out every now and again. He has already had job offers from all over the world. I am guessing they keep track of colleges and look at grades along with many other things. He is accepting the offer from Arizona, or should I say, he is going to visit to do an in-person interview and evaluation. There are too many words I have to look up after talking with Jacob about his career choice. Jacob is a lot of work to talk to." I smile.

I hand Noah the last two bowls, and we head for the living room. We only missed about forty-five minutes. Not a big deal. I have seen this movie so many times.

The movie is soon over, and we are all turning in. I have been waiting for my comfortable bed all day. The nap I took earlier was just what it was, a nap, not really gratifying. Although the sofa is very comfy, I love my bed. It feels like a nest.

I work my way upstairs with everyone after saying our good nights to each other. I flip the switch to the ceiling fan lights, and I turn to talk to Noah. I see Joe and Sarah are on their way upstairs as well as Mother and Father. I ask Mother and Father if we all are getting tucked in for the night. They kiddingly say they want to do a room inspection before we all go to bed. My entire family filters their way into my room. I turn the corner of the stairwell.

"Why are all these mattresses here?"

"When we were kids we would bring our pillows and blankets to sleep on the floor when we wanted to watch a movie in the living room. Then we would have what my parents called a sleepover movie night."

"I'm not getting sleep tonight either, am I?"

As I get closer to the mattresses that are bunched together, I see a pyramid of pillows with a tiny velvet maroon box.

Surprise Sleepover

*M*y eyes fill with tears. Everyone is quiet. I reach for the velvet maroon box from the top of the pillows, and Noah reaches quickly. He takes the box, and I pull my hand back slowly.

All eyes are on Noah and me. It is so quiet. I hear a horse from the barn whiney. I am so excited; it's my turn. We have been dating only a year, I think or maybe it's more. Oh, I don't know. I cannot even think right now.

Noah opens the box slowly and asks me to marry him. He has tears in his eyes, and I am speechless. I reach out again. He takes the ring out of the box. It is a beautiful white gold ring with the largest diamond I have ever seen. Noah tells me, "This is a five-karat princess-cut diamond. I wanted to get you the princess cut. After all, you are my princess, and I knew from the first time I saw you that you are the one for me. You are special to me. Rebekah, I wanted you to have something as vibrant, bold, and beautiful—free spirited as you are. I would love to be your husband if you would kindly say yes."

I look around the room to find Mother and Father in the crowd of family that has circled. I feel Noah take my hand and place the ring on my ring finger of my left hand. He says softly, "You have not answered me." He smiles.

My brothers are yelling my name to answer Noah. "Rebekah, say you do. Say something! Rebekah, what are you waiting for! Rebekah, that diamond is huge. Why are you hesitant, Rebekah?"

"Yes," I say. "Yes."

Everyone yells and hugs Noah and me. My sisters are jumping with excitement.

After they calm down and everyone is done admiring my ring, they scatter to different bathrooms to get ready for bed, then they return to their mattresses around Noah and me. Mother and Father say, "Now I see why you boys were making so much noise earlier. You were moving the mattresses to the second floor from the third floor to have a sleepover in Rebekah's room."

The excitement is over. Mother and Father are in the far corner of the room with Sarah. I just wonder what they are up to now. The secrecy in this family makes me so curious when I am not a part of it.

Noah continues to explain what happened the night he came to the house to surprise me. "I asked your father for your hand, not that I needed to. Your father said that I was very gracious in asking. Your brothers gave me their blessing and added that it would be fine to ask you Christmas or New Year as they did not mind. I thought it would be nice to propose at a time that would be special to us since your brothers proposed on holidays, so I picked tonight, a few days after Thanksgiving and more than a handful of days before Christmas."

I smile and tell him, "I will remember this day as long as I live." I give him a kiss and a hug and told him I loved him, that he was my prince. Noah hugged me even tighter; he told me he loves me too.

Everyone is filtering back into Rachel and my room as they get comfortable on their mattresses. The girls hand me a pen and a notebook. I am confused, "What is this for?"

Noah whispers to me, "I would like to set the wedding date for Christmas!"

I yell with a smile, "Christmas! This Christmas? No sleep tonight either? Can't we do this tomorrow? Well, I guess technically it is tomorrow. This Christmas! Let's be serious!"

Ava explains, "No, silly. Christmas is just around the corner. No one can have a wedding planned that quickly."

Gabby offers up the Grilling Post for both the wedding and the reception. Sounds like an auction; everyone is throwing around ideas to help plan the wedding and reception. Ava adds, "There is also the top of the barn. We would need a caterer."

Sarah offers her services with the Grilling Post, "I got this! Here is what I propose: I can write up different ways to use Gabby's Grilling Post. You can do as Gabby offers. You could use the Grilling Post staff—waiters, waitresses—in the top of our barn. I have access to chandeliers to hang from the rafters of our barn. The boys could load the tables and chairs from the Grilling Post pavilion and transport them to our barn."

Gabby graciously comments, "Yes, you can use anything you need from the Grilling Post wedding venue, even the Grilling Post itself."

Sophia wants to do the centerpieces for the table. She has already showed us one she is doing for Gabby's parents' retirement/going-away party. "They are beautiful," Gabby states.

I give Sophia a definite yes on the centerpieces, and she is drawing some things up with a list of different flowers, vines, and sticks she will need. She says she will show me some ideas tomorrow.

The guys are talking to Noah about the wedding. Which one of them is the best man? They are laughing and carrying on like a bunch of schoolboys.

Ava is looking at the Grilling Post menu for brides and compliments Gabby on being able to do anything from the original menu for a wedding. Gabby agrees, "Anything goes, it's for my sister-in-law! Rebekah is the last of the Sawyers to get married. This is special. There will be no more weddings after Rebekah is married." Ava and Gabby are talking first course, second course, main meal, and desserts, besides the wedding cake.

Joe mentions Mother would more than likely want to make your wedding cake. "Tomorrow, Mother will be checking the Internet and her cookbooks for fancy recipes."

I stop Joe. "There is no way Mother is baking my cake when I need her and everyone else in this family to help me get ready on my wedding day. She is not worrying about a wedding cake. Maybe Rachel could contact one of her friends in New York to come to our ranch and bake the cake instead of Mother doing it. This is not what I want the mother of the bride to do."

My mother's eyes fill with tears, and she is telling everyone she wants to do the wedding cake. "You are the last of my children to get married. I want to do it."

Rachel tries to reason with Mother to make it easy on her. "I will contact my friend from New York to help. Mother, you may be the one to show the pastry chef from New York a few things about baking country style."

I look to Mother and say, "Would that be okay if Rachel does that? I do not want you running around worrying about a cake the day of the wedding when you are needed for pictures with Noah and me, not to mention I would like other pictures with family throughout the property. I want you to enjoy my special day. You are the mother of the bride! You need to help me get ready for my special day," I say excitedly.

Mother looks to Rachel and understands that the bride's mother should do absolutely nothing the day of the wedding and agrees. "Tell your friend they can have the entire responsibility of Rebekah's wedding cake."

I tell Mother she can design and choose the flavor of the cake as Mother suggests she will look on the Internet to find ideas for the perfect cake and cupcakes for the wedding.

Father agrees with me about sleep the rest of the night and states he and Mother are heading to bed. The guys laugh. I smile as I look at my father, and he looks like he has a tear in his eye. After all, I am the last to be married. Father and Mother are off to bed as I sincerely let my family know, "Love you, guys."

I am back with my sisters who are jotting notes and scribbling a dress. "Rachel! You are going to design my dress for my wedding?"

"Yes," Rachel confirms with a smile and a nod. "This dress is on me. It's been a while since you told me what you wanted in a dress. Let's see if I can remember all the details from when we were kids. Has it changed at all?"

As she looks at me, her pencil stops, eraser in her mouth. I shake my head no and tell her, "It's the same."

Rachel goes on to tell me how rare and one of a kind my dress will be. "You do know, no one will have the dress you have. Isn't that special? I will show it online to the public with you in it, of course, only after I design it for you and you wear it. This will happen the day after your wedding. Is that okay?"

I say, "Yes, I am wearing it first. What do you mean with me in it online?"

Rachel says, "I can get you my photographer that does my photo shoots. What I will do is ask them to do your wedding as the photo shoot. Then when my photographer is finished, she can place them online twenty-four to forty-eight hours after your wedding, and you will have your pictures as well."

I am getting anxious almost on the brink of anxiety thinking about all of this. I feel as though things are happening so fast. My conscience is acting a little schizophrenic. I look at Rachel then to everyone in the room. I thank them for all they are doing to help.

Noah says, "We are not on a budget." I look at him from over my sisters and yell, "A budget! What?"

He laughs and says, "No. You do what we need done and just give me the bills. You tell me what time the ceremony is, and I will be there. This is all you, unless you need my help with anything, you know all you have to do is ask."

My brothers tell him that is good he laid the law down. "Rebekah, you better just go with it. Noah just told you how it is," Jeremiah says as the guys are all laughing.

Sophia looks at Jeremiah and Noah in a silly way and begins a pillow fight. Goose feathers are flying everywhere. Noah is trying to step back from the pillow fight, and Sarah and Rachel are slamming him with the pillows. Noah is telling them, "Wait, this is not fair. I cannot fight you girls back. You are not supposed to be overexerting yourselves, and this pillow fight is—" And he is down. Poor Noah never had a chance.

We all worked up an appetite and head to the kitchen. We have to be quiet as Mother and Father are in bed. We sneak down the stairs and notice the light from the stove is on. Mother and Father are in the kitchen. "We could not sleep with the exciting news even though we are tired, so we decided to sit here for a while and talk, drinking a cup of warm milk, thinking it would relax us, then we heard what sounded like a pillow fight going on upstairs for the past thirty minutes, and we are sitting here thinking about how much fun you are all having up there, hopeful not to hurt Sarah or Rachel in the process."

Sophia says, "Sarah and Rachel are fine. It's Noah I would be worried about," as Sarah and Rachel are laughing and telling Mother, "We ganged up on him. We knew he was not going to swing a pillow at us."

Noah tells Mother and Father he never had a chance. This was one pillow fight that was not fair, and they ganged up on him using Sarah and Rachel so he could not fight back. He laughs, and he admits he was actually afraid, admitting he would not be certain if it were Rebekah or Rachel, so he played it safe so no one got hurt.

Everyone is giving their side of the story, talking about how the pillow fight started as they are digging through the refrigerator and cupboards, heating things up in the microwave and making toast.

Mother and Father smile as Mother states, "Everyone was so tired only a few hours ago. Its 2:37 a.m., and we are all up and wide awake."

I confess, and throw Noah under the bus, "It's all Noah's fault."

The girls are all laughing and blaming Noah for not being able to sleep. Noah is trying to defend himself and my brothers kick in to defend him.

As I go to the stairs, the guys are going outside to feed the animals, take a shower, then come to bed. Mother and Father agree it's been a long, exciting night as both our parents make their way to the living room and lay on the double large recliner. The guys change into their work clothes and go to the barn to feed the animals.

My sisters and I make our way back up to the room to go to sleep. Finally, the excitement is over, and we can sleep. I toss and turn, asking if anyone is awake. Ava, Sophia, and Sarah say, "Yes." We just start talking until there is only Ava and I left talking. An old house like this one holds a lot of space to hear what is going on when the house is quiet at night.

I hear the sound of showers throughout the house. I hear the shower in Joe's room, and the shower in our room is busy as I catch a glimpse of Noah running in there. Joshua and Jacob must have taken a shower in the barn bathroom because they are here with their wives, smelling like a rose. The shower on the third floor is running; that is Jeremiah. It is that time in the morning when I should be getting up, but I can't. I am too tired. I smell the coffee brewing. I close my eyes and think what a busy house since Rachel and Jackson are home, not to mention Noah's arrival.

I get awake, hoping I was sleeping for a few hours. I tiptoe out of my room full of family, down the stairs to the kitchen, and I peek around the corner of the dining room to see Mother and Father still lying on the recliner at the far end of the living room. I am thirsty for a glass of milk of which I quietly drink and head back up to sleep as I see the clock on the oven says 10:00 a.m.

I make my way through the mattresses, reach my bed, and I hear Noah talking in his sleep. I lay on the side, gazing at Noah, listening to him talk and giggle in his sleep. I cannot make out the words; it sure is silly to him.

I lay back on my pillow, and I close my eyes. I feel someone close to me as if they are in my face. I open my eyes to see Noah. He tells me he is going to the barn to saddle up and head out with my brothers to go for a ride till we need them at the restaurant later to hang some sort of fabric Rachel was chatting about. He gives me a hug and a peck on my cheek, and down the stairs with my brothers he goes.

I was lying in bed, looking at my ring, holding my hand in the air to let the sun hit it, making a beautiful rainbow color of light on the ceiling, when a pillow comes from the floor and knocks my hand to my bed. I grab the pillow, stand on my bed, and look at Rachel and the girls lying on the floor, smiling and staring back at me. I ask, "What was that for? I am admiring the rest of my life."

Sophia guffawed, "I told you he felt a lot more then you were giving him credit for. He professed his love for you last night in front of your entire family. I am guessing this will be a long engagement. According to you, we all got married so quickly."

"I guess we spent more time together in the past year than I thought," I sighed as I make my bed and wondered if they would be sleeping in my room again tonight.

We get up, make our beds as everyone runs in and out of the bathroom, doing their makeup and hair, getting dressed. In about two hours, we head downstairs to make breakfast for Mother, Father, and ourselves. We notice Mother and Father are still on the chair, sleeping. We are over, surrounding the chair. Ava reaches to turn the lamp on, and Father says, "It's all right. We deserve to sleep in some days, and today seemed like a pretty good day to do it. We should have known after the boys huddled around us, like you are doing, we should have gotten up."

We laugh and giggle, swooning in with hugs. I am helping fold covers and put the recliner in the upright position. Sarah went to the kitchen to start the pancakes with blueberries, Ava is getting the drinks Rachel is setting the table, and I am washing the coffeepot to make coffee again for the third time today. Sophia is feeding the kitties as they made their way to the veranda.

Mother and Father ask what is on our list of things to do today. Sarah says, "We need to run by the restaurant to grab the information mail outs for the bride and grooms weddings that are coming up in two months. Some brides are visual, and some just need to be e-mailed their information from the Grilling Post."

Gabby says, "We need to stop in before the restaurant opens for the day. I need to speak to the staff about the retirement/going-away party for my parents. They need to start a little early today. Sarah let them know when you call them that they will be paid for coming in early today."

Sarah says, "Sure thing, Gabs. I will get on that right after breakfast."

Everyone is eating, chatting on about the day and what needs to be done.

PLANNING

*A*fter breakfast, we are in my room, looking over the guest list, dates, and decorations for Gabby's parents' retirement/going-away party. Gabby is thinking the fifteenth of December for her parents' party. The date is closer than one would hope. The guest list count is fifty. Gabby is wondering which invitations to use. She has it narrowed down to two. Ava, Sophia, and Sarah look at both invitations and suggest she use both. "Why should you have to pick?"

Rachel comments, "Yes, why pick one when you can send both?"

Gabby likes that idea! Gabby hands the address book, invitations, and guest list to me. Gabby smiles; she sets me up with a black gel pen and directions to the Grilling Post. She tells me she likes my handwriting, and these invites must go out today.

I take the two boxes of invitations from her. I address the envelopes first, complete the details of the party on the invitations. The response cards I place with the small response envelopes and the slip of paper with the directions to the party inside the large envelope. I comment, "This is a lot of weight in the envelope. It's going to cost a fortune to send these out."

Gabby remarks with a smile, "I thought of that and wondered if it would have been cheaper and easier to e-mail guests with a nice animated invitation?"

Sarah comments, "I should work on that, possibly incorporate that into my internet site business."

Sophia has pictures of the centerpieces from many angles to get Gabby's approval. Sophia is stating her case that the original plan has changed a bit since the season is winter. She decided to go with different silks to be festive for the holiday season. She also adds she checked with Sarah on the lace tops for the white linens and the beautiful shade is that of a deep candy-apple red. Sophia explains the centerpieces are still tall, but the arrangement at the top has changed to draping holly sprigs with red berries, a few sticks of white lights, white garland with gold tips on a long flexible stick, along with gorgeous poinsettias to match the candy-apple lace on the white linens. The glass vases are filled with glistening shredded white Styrofoam to look like snow.

Gabby has the pictures all lying on the floor in my room. Gabby is interested in how many Sophia has made so far, wondering about the length of time she needs to complete the amount that is needed. "Sophia, how many have you completed?"

Sophia states, "I have six completed with ten more to go. You wanted one in the center of each dining table, two at the gift table, four down the center of the buffet, two on either side of the bar, and one on the dessert table, which makes sixteen. Question is, do you like them? I need to order more silks and a few other things. I have a short list for the hobby shop in my handbag so I can order to finish them in time."

Gabby states, "I love them! They are beautiful, so elegant and tastefully done. I want to thank you for your hard work. I want to thank all for helping me put this together." Gabby hugs everyone.

Ava and Sarah are reviewing the table placement, along with the guest-seating chart. Ava's asking, "Is there anyone that should not sit with someone else. Does everyone get along?"

Gabby answers, "Mix friends with the family so they will get to know everyone."

"That sounds good," Ava said with a laugh.

Sarah and Gabby are looking at the menu. They are discussing what should already be on the tables, what should come with the first course, the second course, and so on to get a good menu for the dinner party. The party and everything around it is coming together. Sophia asks, "Gabby, you should get the pictures of the grand opening of the Grilling Post and a few other candid and eventful photos of your parent's life when they were first together. The pictures then will go on a table under glass so everyone can see them as they are walking in."

Sarah ordered champagne, wine, and some popular mixers with many flavors of microbrewed beer. Gabby is on the phone with the chef. She is talking to her about the date and time of the dinner party. Sarah calls Allianna, head of the wait staff. She ends the call by saying Gabby will speak with them about details when they arrive.

Sarah is on to the next call to the hobby shop to order all the things Sophia will need to finish the centerpieces. Sarah eagerly confronts Sophia for her list of items needed to finish the centerpieces for the dinner party for Gabby's parents. Sarah is talking to the person on the phone, placing Sophia's order. She notifies them, "Charge it on the account for the Grilling Post and Sophia will be by to pick it up later today say around threeish." She says her thank you and goodbyes; she is on her way downstairs to ask our parents to call Gabby's parents to plan a decoy, then bring them to the Grilling Post for their party. Sarah gives them the information of the party. Our parents enjoy Gabby's parents and cannot wait to get together with them.

We load up in the Suburban to head out to the Grilling Post. Gabby makes a quick stop at the post office so I can get the invitations in the mail for her. I hand the invitations to the postmaster, Tiana Rae, one of my childhood friends. "These will go out today! How are you? We need to do lunch and catch up." I thank Tiana, "Yes, I agree, time just doesn't stop. It seems like yesterday we were in detention together after the water incident in the bathroom." We both giggle and say goodbye. When I reach Gabby, I notify her, "The invites made it to get out in the mail today."

Gabby is relieved. She realizes there is no time to waste. "The party will be here before you know it."

We arrive at the restaurant. We scatter to start checking things out. Gabby says the staff will soon be here so she can speak with them about catering the party December 15, Sunday after church. Sarah has a schematic of the restaurant and the guest list. She finishes the placement of the guests at the tables, places it in her schedule book to have Gabby take a look at it later.

It is up to us to get some ideas of elegant decorations for this retirement/going-away party. Sarah says the Christmas tree will be up, so that will add to the decor. Sophia says, "I have a suggestion."

We wait to hear what she has to say.

Sophia continues, "In some cases, less is more, if you know what I mean."

We look at her, puzzled.

"What I mean is we have this tree that will match the swag for the bar and tall centerpieces for the tables, not to mention the candy apple-red overlays on the white linens. And with the white sheers the guys will be hanging, it will all come together make a festive tastefully decorated party. Wait until the guys come. You will see what I mean."

The staff and chef arrive. They gather around the four tables at the back of the room. Sarah and Gabby join them. Gabby is speaking to the staff about wearing a little more than a T-shirt with their name ironed on the top front and the Grilling Post in big letters on the back. They are smiling at each other as Gabby informs the staff, "I am sure you have heard I will be managing the business January 1 of the New Year." She hands them a book of restaurant uniforms and says, "We all need to agree to disagree on more appropriate attire for you. I need you to be comfortable but more professional. The uniform company is allowing us to request different types of clothing so you may all try it on to see how it fits before we order. I know we will not be in the new outfits right away, but I would like to be in them before the end of January if not the beginning of February."

Everyone is nodding their heads yes with a big smile. "The business will purchase all the outfits you will need. I am having your name embroidered on the top left under the Grilling Post, so you will not have to wear a pin with your name on it. I was also thinking maybe in the summer to wear something that is tasteful, comfortable but cooler, a nice dress short or a nice length skirt from this catalog as well. You think about it and let me know. I am not sure for the cook staff, but with the wait staff, I was thinking this could happen.

"Everyone, let me know. You can send me a text or a voicemail about what you think about the new uniforms. We have a great staff, and we are a high-end restaurant. I just want us to look the part. Our next meeting is the fourth of December. Everyone's thoughts are important to me. December 4, more information will be given to you. I would also like you to voice your thoughts as well. I cannot run a restaurant without input from staff that sees things firsthand. Write things down, which we will discuss and find solutions for."

Gabby goes on to tell the staff why she has called them to the restaurant. "I called you here today because I am planning a going-away/retirement party for my parents. I need your help to pull this off. You know what you do when there is a wedding on a Saturday at the pavilion. I am asking for a Sunday with an incentive, of course, because it is a day you would normally have off. It will be December 15.

"I am also paying you your regular rate plus double time and a half to work and to attend the party. Your time is precious as well. I want to start off our relationship as manager and employees on a good note. I respect what you do. Everyone at this business is an asset and makes this restaurant run smoothly. I know some of you have worked with my parents a long time and some not as long as others. I would like you to make and serve dinner, which will probably take a few hours, and then during dinner, it should only be an hour. I want all of you to join us.

"What I am suggesting is to make the chef and kitchen help figure out and keep things on warm or in ovens till we need it. The wait staff can set things up to make it is possible for you all to join us as well. Everyone will receive a paycheck for working this party. My family and I will help during the evening where we can. There are ten plus in my immediate family, and we will not step foot in the kitchen to be in anyone's way unless asked by the chef. A lot of us can help clear tables and put dishes in the dishwasher, which should not take long. We should not be in anyone's way since the dishwasher is just inside to the left of the 'IN' door to the kitchen.

"Oh, yeah, I have hired DJ Jazzy to play for the night. She will be here as long as we want her. My parents have always treated you fairly, and I want to do the same."

My brothers, Jackson and Noah arrive. Sarah asks them to hang and swag white sheer long fabric going from the two far back corners of the dance floor ceiling to meeting in the center of the ceiling before the dining room with bright white twinkle lights lying in the fabric. It is elegant. Sarah looks at Gabby; they both think one should be hung in the middle to meet the length of the other two. Noah and Jackson put the lights in the sheer, while Jeremiah and Jacob hang the last sheer. "Now that looks perfect," Gabby says.

Gabby hears Chef Shay give her opinion: "The sheer swags look great! I just wanted you to know that everyone working tonight will be working your parents' party. It would be an honor to cook and serve your parents and their guests. Your parents will be missed."

The chef hands Gabby bags of dinner for tonight. Sarah called the house and asked Mother not to cook. Gabby is bringing a surprise from the Grilling Post. Father and our brothers love ribs. Gabby is overjoyed and thanks the chef.

We gather at the door of the Grilling Post. Gabby stops and looks back at the draped sheers with lights one last time before we leave. We all agree it looks elegant and tasteful. "Less is more."

Gabby smiles at Sophia. "You are correct about decorating."

Sophia hears her and smiles.

We are on our way out as the first reservations for the start of the evening dinner arrive, and the hostess is seating them. Gabby hands the two bags of food to Jeremiah and Joe; she is checking with the Grilling Post staff to make sure everyone is okay, thanking them again. As she is leaving the establishment, she tells everyone to have a great night.

Shay hands Gabby the last three bags of food, and we are in the Suburban and on our way home. I admit, "I am ready for a nap. It has been a long two days rolled into one. I guess balloons are overrated when Sophia's around."

Sophia says, "Balloons are for kids' parties. I will show you when we have a fifth birthday party for our additions to our family."

Rachel looks at Sophia and laughs. "Five years old? Let's wait until these little people are born, then we plan."

The smell of ribs with garlic broccoli noodles and sweet rolls fills the Suburban on the way home. "Chef Shay came into the Grilling Post kitchen last night and loaded the smoker with ribs for today's special."

Rachel has a call on her cell phone from her New York office. We hear Rachel in her business voice tell them what needs to be done, that she can be on the first plane out in the morning. I look at Sarah, and Rachel's tone is stern with a growl to it. Sarah, Ava, Gabby, Sophia, and I are all quiet, wondering what is happening and why Rachel has to fly to New York.

Rachel gets off the phone. We reach the driveway, and Ava pulls over. I ask, "Why the flight to New York?"

She starts to explain. "I knew this was going to happen. I should not have gone until everything was taken care of."

We all ask, "What is taking care of?"

"My clothing line will no longer be in New York. It is moving to Italy. I should say the design line of clothes I am selling to Italy. I have changed to

166

designing wedding dresses. Not sure if I told anyone. I am ranting like everyone should know."

Rachel apologizes. "It is not a ridiculous amount of money, just a few measly dollars. I am not a *big*-name designer, but I am one of many small-name designers. I like working one-on-one with the client. I will design for a company out of New York. The fashion world knows my passion is wedding dresses.

"I actually have twenty-one wedding dresses sketched. Each sketched dress is unique, elegant, and breathtaking when you see it for the first time. I will be working directly with the client. No one dress is the same, and I get to know the bride. Like you, Rebekah, I can put the dress in magazines and on my website after the date of the wedding is over to ensure the wedding takes place and I abide by the contract of the sketch to the client. Then and only then the world will have access to that particular dress.

"There are a lot of legalities in this business. I will call my lawyer to have her look over the paper I did not sign, then I will have her scan it in so I receive it in an e-mail, and I perhaps won't have to take the jet to New York."

"So the jet is yours?" I ask.

"Yes," Rachel replies. "It is Jackson and mine. We will be selling it because the upkeep is expensive.

Then there is the cost of the pilot. We are going to have a baby and remodel the summerhouse. We do not need a jet."

Rachel laughs. "Jackson and I will have to settle for 'first class on a commercial fight.'"

As she smiles, we are all making and poking fun of her uppity antics. I tell her, "Your amusing behavior is not suited to hang around with us ranchers." I nudge her, and we are all carrying on joking around that she is too high-class for us to be hanging out with her.

We reach the farmhouse, park Father's Suburban, and run into the house. Rachel and I enter the house first. I see Noah hesitate until Jackson makes his move. I look at Sarah and tell her, "This could be interesting with Noah."

We both laugh. I know Sarah is up for some trickery. Rachel is telling Jackson of the phone call she received; Jackson will check the e-mail to make sure she is aware when the paper arrives so she can sign it and get it back to the lawyer. Jackson adds, "The moving crew will be bringing those few things you could not leave New York without. I figured we do not need to travel back to New York just to grab those few pieces of furniture you wanted to keep, so I arranged for the Sea-to-Sea Movers to do it for us. They should be arriving any day now."

Rachel thanks Jackson for doing that and states, "I really do not want to go back to the big apple if I do not need to." She smiles at Jackson from across the room, making her way to the door to say her good-byes to her family, and she will probably see them sometime this week. "I would love to visit to see any changes you made to your homes, even something as little as the décor. Since I am home, I need to catch up on the latest country decor."

Ava, Sophia, Sarah, and Gabby smile, hug Rachel and Jackson, telling them, "Glad you are home, and you can visit anytime."

Everyone is saying goodbye. They all agree it won't be long and Christmas will be here. Father states we will all see each other throughout the days ahead. The family is here for three weeks if not longer. My brothers are tugging at their wives toward their SUVs to get back to their cabins on opposite corners of the ranch. Finally, everyone is loaded, and they head out the driveway in four different directions.

Jackson talks to Noah about moving to the third floor after the New Year's holiday. Jackson says, "I have a four-stages-of-life bed on order. That should be coming beginning of February." Jackson is excited.

Noah tells Jackson, "I can help you get it up the stairs and together if you like."

Jackson states, "Most definitely! I am sure it will be a project even with the directions."

Noah and Jackson are in the living room with Father. Mother, Rachel, and I are in the kitchen, cleaning up, placing some dishes in the dishwasher.

Rachel grabs her laptop and starts checking her e-mail. Jackson and Noah are talking with Father about the pregnant cattle in the barn. Mother picks up her book and is looking for her glasses. She finds them on the end table by the lamp. I go upstairs to grab my laptop from my room. I check to see if I need to complete any other work for my classes. If the professor placed a list of things I have to complete, I will start them to hopefully complete them sooner rather than later. One more month of online sessions and I will have my associate's degree for general business accounting along with some other degree. I start my college courses with Noah the end of February.

E-MAILS AND
TEXT MESSAGES

I am looking over my list of Internet homework from my professor. There is a bubble e-mail notification from Sophia. As I open the e-mail, I notice Sophia sent an e-mail with a few pictures of centerpieces she made for my wedding. I like the tall one with white wisteria, pussy willows, ivy greens, white calla lilies, and red rosebuds accented with baby's breath, not to mention the beautifully placed pearl strands throughout the centerpieces dangling from different areas of the mass bouquet at the top of the tall vase. Sophia made this one out of silks; it is beautiful, and it looks so real. She also gives a preview of the boutonnieres for my father and brothers, bouquets for my sisters, and the cascading bridal bouquet, which is breathtakingly sensational. Seeing the flowers makes me anxious for my wedding.

I return Sophia's e-mail:

Sophia,

The centerpieces are beautiful. Which are cheaper; the silks that look fantastically real or the fresh cut flowers? The silks are just fine if it is easier. I know you would be able to work on them to get them done sooner if they were silk. You could store them in my room under a piece of plastic so they stay clean until the wedding. Let me know your thoughts.

Thank you again for doing this for Noah and me!

Love Ya',
Rebekah

Rebekah then presses send, and the e-mail is sent to Sophia.

Sophia has been helping her family at the Flowering Cactus all her life; it is something she has enjoyed. She has the knowledge of doing the most spectacular arrangements of flowers for events any-one has ever seen without thought. She can do amazing things with flowers. I know my wedding is in good hands. With Sophia creating my flowers, I have nothing to worry about.

I scroll through my e-mails from the latest to the most recent and notice another e-mail from Sophia she typed just an hour ago. This is the e-mail Sophia wrote:

Rebekah,

Jeremiah got accepted to a residency in Texas. He will be there for 5 years.

The faculty and staff want him to fly out to do a face-to-face meet and greet, tour their facility and they will help find a place for him and his family to live until the residency is over.

Jeremiah e-mailed the Human Resources Department and is waiting for them to return an e-mail with information on a flight and other things.

We will come to the farm house to tell Joe and Abigail sometime this week when Jeremiah gets that e-mail and we know what is happening so he can deliver all the information at one time. Jeremiah also applied for a fellowship and is looking at a Cardiologists private practice in San Diego, California. He wrote a letter to the fellowship site stating he is just starting his residency and would like to further his goal of becoming a Cardiologist by doing his fellowship at their private practice for a year. Jeremiah attached it to his application. If he goes to Texas I will be traveling with him. The only thing is we will not be able to come home all the time. I would think the holidays but then I wonder if he could get the time off. We will cross that bridge when we come to it. He applied other places but speaks highly of San Diego. So we will see. Jeremiah and I will see you and the family in a few days.

I apologize for my jumbled thoughts.

Love,
Sophia

Rebekah returns an e-mail to Sophia:

Sophia,

Five years will fly by. Who knows, you may like Texas. They have horses there too ya know. Lol

I am sensing you have mixed feelings about this residency and fellowship.

You and Jeremiah are very supportive of each other. Things will be great! You knew in the field and career choices you both made there would be some sacrifices along the way. Staying in Texas over the holidays could be one of those many sacrifices although they do know his family lives in Wyoming so just wait and see, they may surprise you.

You will also be making new friends and having dinner parties with doctors. Rubbing elbows with some pretty important people. You will be learning to be the wife of a doctor as Jeremiah learns to be a little more than a doctor.

Personally the move and time would be socializing. That is just another challenge you will take on. I have never known you to back away from a challenge... either one of you. I think it is exciting.

One day you and Jeremiah will look back when you have your own practice or whatever it is you both decide to do and think you have come a long way from how things used to be and to only know it gets better and easier with every day you both are doing what you love, saving lives.

Mother always says things work out and Father with his turn the negative to positive as he is always saying.

They are right ya know. You will be just fine. Lol

Love you both! See you when you guys come over. I will not say a word. You deliver your own thunder.

Talk to ya soon Love ya,
Rebekah

Rebekah is aware Sophia will be replying any moment. She moves on to the next e-mail. This one is from Gabby:

Rebekah,

Jacob received news from Arizona.
Neurophysiology Lab of Arizona would like to do an interview in person with Human resources and they want to show him around the plant/lab.

Jacob is excited he has spoken to the president of the company. He likes how easy it is to talk with him. Sounds like a good place and good people. He needs to fly out in a week or two.

I will stop over in a day or two. I need to speak with you about the retirement party.

I received all the RSVPs back. Everyone will be there. I am so excited!

Love ya See you soon,
Gabby

Rebekah returns Gabby's e-mail:

Hey Gabby!

That is such great news!

I am so happy things are happening so quickly for Jacob. You guys can deliver Jacob's news to the family whenever you get here.

Sure whenever you get a minute just text me with the time and I can let you know if I can take a little time away. Hahahaha

I will make sure I am at the ranch when you plan to come.

Love ya ttyl,
Rebekah

Joshua and Ava stopped by to talk with our parents. They are telling them they sent their information and their credentials to many different businesses who are looking to hire architects to design business high-rises, penthouses, towns/communities, and many types of houses for developments. Ava tells everyone she has received calls that requested information from her. She mailed out information on both her and Joshua. Joshua tells Mother and Father, "We want to get with Rachel and Jackson on the basement plans we have completed. There were little things we had to check on when we showed them the plans for the summer house after Thanksgiving."

I ask, "Where are Rachel and Jackson?"

"Rachel and Jackson are upstairs on the second floor. Not sure if they are napping or just relaxing," Mother says.

I say, "I will run up and see if they have a moment to come down and look at some plans."

Ava thanks me, and I am on my way up the stairs. I am almost to the top of the stairs on the second floor when I hear Rachel say, "If it's a boy, Jackson Ray. If it's a girl, what did you think?"

Jackson then says, "JackieRae."

Rachel says, "Are you serious? Why? Please tell me because it has your name and mine. I thought we were not doing Js."

"JackieRae would be the entire first name. Her middle name would be Savannah," Jackson replies. "You don't like that? I thought you liked Savannah."

"I do. I love the name Savannah, but I thought we would incorporate my mother's name into her name," Rachel immediately comments.

Jackson asks, "What about my mother's name?"

"No, you cannot be serious! Kay?" Rachel then says sternly, "No way."

Jackson then laughs and says, "My mother never liked her name. I doubt she would want her grandchild named after her."

They are now both laughing. I come around the corner and say, "So it will be Jackson Ray if it's a boy and JackieRae Savannah or Abigail Savannah? What about RebekahRae SavannahGail?"

Rachel and Jackson tell me they were bored and started the conversation they said they would never start until three months before the baby is born. Jackson says, "I like RebekahRae SavannahGail. Sounds nice. It's a lot but sounds nice."

Rachel agrees. "If it's a boy, it is definitely Sebastian Jackson. I like that name."

Jackson smiles and reaches for Rachel. "She's going to the doctor for her checkup December 18. She will then be at least fifteen weeks, give or take a couple of days. She did not have time to do a blood draw, which would have told us the sex of the baby sooner."

Rachel says, "I opted out of the blood draw. I figure I can wait. I am too busy to stop every time a doctor wants me to do something. I notified the office I don't want labs. I am not real fond of needles. I know I will be hooked up to all kinds of good stuff the day my child is born, but I don't need any extra early needle sticking any time soon."

Jackson adds, "Rachel has an appointment to tell the sex of the baby near the end of January. She has to be twenty or so weeks along to check."

I ask, "Are you going with Sarah to the doctor? I am pretty sure Sarah has an appointment December 18."

Rachel mentions, "I will contact Sarah to ask her when her appointment date and time is since we see the same provider. This is just a checkup." Rachel grabs her phone and starts texting Sarah.

On our way to the kitchen, I tell them, "Joshua and Ava are in the kitchen, wanting you to look at plans. I think they said they completed the basement and would like you to okay a few other things with the rest of the summer kitchen plans."

Rachel says, "I am so excited about getting the summer kitchen remodeled. I cannot wait to see what they have done."

Ava brings the long cylinder to the dining room, pops the lid off the one end, and slides the plans out onto the table. Ava rolls them out, everyone holding on to a corner as Ava starts the renovation pitch. Joshua started with the office in the basement. The renovations are completed to perfection on the large layout of the office. Rachel and Jackson are pleased.

Ava goes on to the next page as they flip to the first floor of the summer kitchen. The kitchen plans include all the changes Rachel wanted. Off the kitchen is the living room, a master bedroom with full bath. Rachel loves everything they have done to make this small space a home. To the back of the living room, there are two bedrooms that share a full bathroom. Jackson loves these additions as well. Rachel is asking if there can be a wraparound porch with a placement for a grill top. Joshua says, "We will work on that."

Ava smiles and says, "Not a problem."

Rachel, Jackson, Ava, and Joshua, still talking about the plans, make their way to our parents at the bar in the kitchen. Our parents ask how the plans are coming along. Joshua says, "Looks like Ava has nailed the basement, and the first floor is looking good too!"

I am looking at the horses in the pasture through the window of the kitchen, and they see something that is bringing them to the fence by the edge of the driveway. I see Gabby and Jacob ride up to the house. They tie their horses to the post and sit on the porch with the collies. Our family walks out to join them. Sophia and Jeremiah are tying their horses at the other end of the post. Jeremiah looks to everyone. "How is everyone doing?" He goes on to say, "We rode over to speak with Mother and Father about leaving the state for a few years."

Mother and Father look at each other. Father says, "Jeremiah, who picked you to do your residency and where, California, Pennsylvania, Nebraska, Tennessee?"

Sophia blurted out, "Texas! We will be gone for five long years. We are not sure if we will be able to get home for any holidays."

Just then, Jeremiah reaches out to Sophia, hugs her, and explains, "Sophia is a little uneasy about the five years in Texas for my residency, then I do my fellowship in California. I keep telling her we will be fine, that she will be so busy with her studies and making new friends, the five years will fly by quickly. When it comes time to leave, she will have a hard time leaving there, like leaving the ranch."

Father says, "Sophia, Jeremiah is right, you know. Time will fly by, and before you know it, you will be home, wishing you were back in Texas and California with your friends you made, dinner parties you threw, dinner parties you attended. Enjoy this part of your life. This is all a new experience for both of you."

We all cozy up on the veranda with coffee, hot chocolate, and the blankets I brought out from the back of the sofa in the living room. Mother is telling Sophia and Jeremiah, "This journey you two are about to embark on is going to be one you will always remember as a wonderful time away, although you will only be gone a short time. What a fantastic experience. What a wonderful time alone without family, making new friends and meeting all types of people. I think you will have a wonderful time. We are only a phone call away."

Mother smiles, reaches out for Sophia's hand and holds tight. "It will not be all that long, and you will be back to do what it is you two do best—saving lives and helping people.

"Sophia, did you call your parents."

Jeremiah is explaining, "When Sophia comes, we will check the houses together." He smiles and gets a smile back from Sophia.

Sophia does not want to leave everyone, although she knows she has to. Sophia says while holding Mother's hand, "I spoke to my parents briefly. You know my parents. You have to go and give Jeremiah support, and he will help you figure out how to stay where you are to be. That is what my parents tell me. They are not real personable or close-knit like you and your children are. I know they love me. They are just not affectionate, emotional parents. Thank you, Abigail, for being loving and not afraid to show affection."

Mother says, "Sophia, dear, don't be too hard on your parents. Your parents are good people. Growing up, they may have not had the show of love and affection as other children may have. When you are away, call your parents more. It may bring them around since they cannot see you every day."

Sophia smiles and hugs Mother.

Gabby and Jacob mention the opportunity Jacob has in Arizona to tour a facility. Jacob will be flying at the end of the week as well. Jacob is telling everyone he will probably have to move; not real sure if working remotely is an option. Mother and Father smile. Jacob admits, "I know we may probably have to move sooner rather than later. They will talk to me more about their expectations of me when I arrive."

It's a little chilly. We make our way to the living room. Father makes a fresh pot of coffee. Mother calls the Grilling Post and is placing an order for dinner. I can hear Mother say, "Three family size orders of ribs, pulled pork bar-b-q, and seasoned beef. No, no, thank you. Sure, thank you. You have a nice evening as well." Sarah is bringing the food home with her. Sarah had to stop in at the restaurant to check on some important papers for Gabby. Mother has garlic noodles baking in the oven as well as fresh honey-buttered rolls to go with the meats that will be arriving soon.

Noah and I went to look at the summer kitchen before things get rearranged, painted, and construction starts with all Rachel's floor plans. We were chatting about moving the wedding up, possibly in the summer, sometime when we know everyone is home or maybe before everyone leaves. Noah says he is fine with whatever I want to do. I need to speak with Sarah about the wedding dress—privately, of course.

Noah and Rebekah call Gabby to the summer kitchen. As they walk around and comment on the beautiful, rustic accents of the summer kitchen, they inform Gabby, "We want to move the wedding up." I go on rambling about having to speak to the others eventually, but guess I should do it sooner rather than later.

Gabby is fine with moving things along. She says, "I will do what I can with the time and access of resources I have." I show her a picture I found on the Internet of tables covered in white linen, with large bent wrought iron shepherds' hooks that hold chandeliers over the tables.

"You know how much of a chance you are taking putting everything outside without being under cover?" Gabby asked.

"I know. Doesn't it look like a ranch wedding?" I ask her.

"Sure does, but you have to be prepared! All the work, money, and time that go into a wedding spread like that to have it ruined by rain and your guests along with it. Think about that. I am only being practical. Weather is so unpredictable," Gabby explains. "When the photo was taken, they, of course, waited for a lovely day, as depicted here, to make that look possible, but in reality, an outside wedding is weather enabled. You don't want to have to worry about weather. You can make it look just as beautiful inside. Trust me. I talk to a lot of brides when they are looking for venues. They tell me what they want and what they expect from an outdoor wedding. I am blunt and honest. Everything starts outside, but in the end, when paperwork is signed, they are inside or under the pavilion at the Grilling Post."

Noah is thinking and listening on the sidelines, then says, "Rebekah, how about we get married in the barn loft with everyone down below us then move to the second level for the reception? Or we could get married out by the lake then ride everyone into the barn to have hors d'oeuvres before the start of the reception. If it rains, we do the loft wedding. Then we have a backup plan if you want to do something outside, and everyone wins."

"That sounds special," Gabby states. "Rebekah, what do you think?"

"I cannot believe a guy thought of that," I confess. "It is a perfect place for our ceremony. I think it is a wonderful idea to ride guests from the barn to the lake and back again. We have four large wagons. What a great idea, Noah!"

I hug Noah as he goes on to say, "Your brothers took me past there when we went on the rides to exercise the horses. I often wondered why we did not pass the lake when we rode."

I say, "We just had not covered that ground. Our ranch is so large, we would have eventually passed the lake."

Noah says, "If the crisis is over, I want to get back to the barn as I have some work to do out there." He gives me a kiss on my forehead and leaves the house with Father as they walk through the kitchen out onto the veranda heading to the barn.

We see them chatting and carrying on about some plans for after the wedding. Gabby says, "The rest of the girls need to know the wedding is moved up so we can get things moving."

I agree. I ask Gabby, "Do you think you and Jacob will be moving to Arizona?"

"Not sure, but it may be possible. Not right now. Maybe in a week, month, a year. Why? Jacob has a great mind. He told me the facility in Arizona runs tests to evaluate new discoveries for real-world problem-solving," Gabby says. "We did discuss not getting involved in top secret projects to have people hunt him down like in the movies."

We both laugh. "Jacob did say if he is chosen and placed in a group picked to do what he can for the good of people and better the future in this world to finding solutions he will be honored to be in that group. I like the way he thinks," Gabby says as we are back with the family in the kitchen.

I notify everyone, "Noah and I have decided to get married sooner rather than later. With everyone in this family doing their career moves, if I do not plan it soon, we won't have groomsmen and bridesmaids."

My family laughs. I also add, "Mother was right. When the triplets start their careers, their lives will move quickly, and the nest will be almost empty."

Rebekah sees Mother nod her head yes from across the kitchen as she pours another cup of coffee. Mother asks, "How's your dress coming along? Will it be ready soon?"

Rachel chimes in and says, "It will be ready in a few weeks. I sent the design to the seamstress in New York right after Rebekah got engaged. I texted Raven and notified her to be expecting Rebekah's wedding design within the week." Rachel laughs and says, "I added Rebekah's measurements I took while she was dead to the world Mother's dinner bell wouldn't have woken her. I received a text from Raven, she notified me she is ready. Rebekah's dress will be top priority. This was the wedding dress I drew years ago for Rebekah. You don't know how many times I was tempted to throw it to the wedding market, only to rethink that Rebekah will want this dress, and after all these years, she is not that little girl anymore. She's got even bigger dreams."

I commented, "Gee, Rachel, I don't know how big my dreams are, but I can tell you I still love the dress you drew me years ago as a little girl. By the way, did you ever receive the contract through the e-mail to sign for Italy?"

Rachel says, "Yes, the designer in Italy that bought the line gave me a little bonus. I received one million for the rights to my designs. I gave them a signed contract to place their name on the designs and change them a little to make them their own."

Rachel looks at me and adds, "We sold the jet. Although the papers are not signed, we will get that taken care of as soon as the interested party gets back in a few months from their vacation. We would like to invest money in the ranch for Mother and Father and put the rest in a trust for our children."

Jackson asks, "Enough business talk. Is everyone ready for the retirement party at the Grilling Post for Gabby's parents?"

Gabby says, "Yes, everyone at the restaurant knows what has to be done. We have nothing else to do but show up. The staff will get the entire party together from the clean linens on the table the night before to the centerpiece placement on all of the tables. The wait staff will set up the hors d'oeuvres table. Everything has fallen into place. Sophia and I will drop off the centerpieces and swag the night before when the Grilling Post is closed."

Sophia notifies us they are all boxed up and ready to go.

LETTER FROM GRANDMOTHER

I am rattling on about the wedding. Mother tells me to follow her. Mother hands me an envelope she has pulled from an old box on her dresser. I see an old long wrinkled discolored envelope, a little tattered and torn brought to the envelope's limits as it is protecting of its contents. She hands me this, and she sits on the bed. I open it. It is a letter from my grandmother, written to me, and this is what it said:

My Dearest Granddaughter,

I would love nothing more than to hold you in my arms.

Lay your head against my chest, smell that beautiful newborn scent, kiss your forehead and tell you how much I'm going to spoil and love you.

I'd tell you how beautiful you are and how you could be anything in the world so long as you put your heart and mind into it.

I am sorry that I'm not there to give you my love and attention, to help you grow, learn, and to share all my wonderful memories and wisdom.

I must leave this world without meeting you and oh how it breaks my heart.

I have so much I want to share with you; there aren't enough words to express the love I already have for you.

My darling granddaughter, when you crack your first smile, say your first word, crawl for the first time, and take your first steps; please know that I will be there with you. I'll be cheering you on and helping you get back up when you fall.

Your first giggle out loud will bring tears of joy and it will be a sound I'll never forget. I can still hear your mother's first giggle and oh how the time goes by so fast and how quickly our babies grow up.

Your mother is my pride and joy. I know you will be hers too.

As you enter your teenage years remember as beautiful as you are always stay humble and kind.

Do unto others as you wish for others to do unto you.

Be patient with your mother. She knows what is best and although you may not agree sometimes, she too was once a teenager.

As you take that leap finding a man you wish to marry, be sure you find someone who will allow you to be yourself, a man who is gentle and kind yet won't be afraid to fight for you.

You'll know he's the one when his smile has a special light. When you look into his eyes, you will feel like you can look into his soul and you will feel like he can change the world.

The big step in your life, that beautiful day you become a wife and one day a mother.

Thinking and imagining you on your wedding day touching up your make up, straightening your gown, fixing that one strand of hair and wiping your first tear will be all the things I wish I could be there for.

My strong beautiful talented baby girl you will look amazing!

I would tell you how gorgeous you are.

There may come a time in your marriage when you will feel like giving up.

However give it your all and know that every obstacle you overcome with your husband as one will form a bond that can't be broken.

Communication and Trust are the keys to a great marriage.

So as you lift your veil to say, "I do" to the man of your dreams

Make the most of every moment you share my darling girl because life is beautiful. Life is fast, in the blink of an eye you go from the age you are now to 100 in less than 60 seconds, no joke.

So live your life to the fullest and never be afraid to follow your heart and make choices that may sometimes seem impossible.

Tackling your biggest fears is what will make you the best that you can be.

I must say goodbye but know it is not forever. Someday I'll welcome you with open arms and finally hold you, my granddaughter.

Please always remember I am a prayer away and will always be here listening. Watching you take each step of your life. I love you baby!

May your life be filled with love, joy and happiness.

I love you.
Gram

I am in tears, looking at my mother. My voice cracks. "How? What? When did your mother...when did Gram write this? Did Gram write to everyone?"

Mother explained, "Your grandmother, my mother, wrote one for her grandsons and one letter for her granddaughters. She made me promise to give it to each one of her grandchildren before they marry."

"I will cherish this letter the rest of my life." I am excited and sad as I hold it to my chest, hugging it. I hug my mother and thank her. I take my letter to my room and put it on my dresser. Rachel looks my way and makes a heart with her hands then points to me. She knows Mother gave me the letter from our grandmother. Oh, how I wish I could have met my grandparents. I bet they would love this large ranch and to have all these grandchildren. I bet it would be a wonderful time!

Father reminds us daily we must be thankful and embrace our family, and to be with family is a blessing. My mother told me I have the original copy of my gram's letter. My mother was told to copy the letter for her boys and girls, to give the last child the original. I tell my mother I want to put it in a frame so I can see it every day, along with a picture of my grandparents. My mother smiles as a tear comes to her eye. She tells me the original letter written for the boys went to Joshua.

I take Noah back upstairs to show him the letter my grandmother wrote. I ask him when he thought our wedding date should be. "I am worried my brothers won't be able to attend."

Noah sees how saddened I am: "You do realize your brother Jeremiah won't be leaving for at least a month after his return from this big peer-to-peer interview and tour of the hospital. Jacob is only visiting the facility as well, doing his face-to-face interview with the employer, who is interested in your brother's knowledge. Nothing is set in stone yet with either of them. Something could be said the wrong way at the interview not intended or not noticed but taken out of context to how the phrase or one simple little word is interpreted, and it's all over. Let's just plan for May or June, and we can do the ceremony by the lake and reception in the barn. What are your thoughts now that I had you step back from the situation a bit? Look at it as not moving so quickly."

I mention to Noah, "I am thinking of a spring wedding at the lake and reception in the barn."

Noah embraces me and tells me, "Everything will work out. You just wait and see."

So Much to Do

I ask the girls if they want to saddle up and go for a ride. "I need to exercise the horses a little before we have more snow, and I want to chat about a spring wedding. I need to get some fresh air in my brain to clear it some. I must confirm the things we have and things I need, a checklist if you will. Then I want to chat about the retirement party. I need to push my mind in another direction."

Ava, Sophia, Gabby, and I saddle up the horses. The girls observe and comment how tall and huge Duchess is as we ride out across the yard. We can see Rachel and Sarah waving to us from the house. They ask me if we have a date set in stone for the wedding, "I obviously think Noah and I are looking at a spring date, although we have been throwing a few dates around. I really want to make sure my brothers will be home before we do set the date. You know, it's been a few days since I spoke to the guys about their wedding attire. I have to get the men in our family go to the Tall Pines Tuxedo Shop soon."

"When my dress comes in, we can plan a date, hopefully before everyone has to leave and go on their travels and move off the ranch for their careers, although Noah has assured me we can do a spring wedding. I am aiming for May or June. Does that sound reasonable?" I ask.

"It is good you have a target date for your wedding. A wedding is a big deal. You are trying to plan it around your brothers so everyone is here, and most brides are selfish when it comes to planning their wedding. Meaning, they want this date, and that is it. You, Rebekah, on the other hand, want to make sure your entire family will be there," Gabby states a fact.

Ava chimes in, "That is what any bride would want, yes?"

Gabby admits, "I have met a lot of brides, and Sarah can tell you, they get a little temperamental about dates, about family not attending or attending. Most brides want the same date they were engaged. Others want the wedding date to be the first time they met. Then there are others with dates with other meanings to them. The rest of the brides tell Sarah how they would like to have the wedding in July. The bride gives the year and asks if there are any dates open. Not everyone is easy. We try to please everyone as well, which in some cases does not happen. We will do a wedding on the weekday, which is cheaper for some brides, and most do it on the weekday because they don't want certain family members to attend. I am sorry I am rambling on about weddings and you wanted to clear your head."

I say, "That's okay. All of that makes me think I could be an impossible bride, but I'm not."

"Oh, no, not at all. Your situation is reasonable," Gabby says. "Totally different than what Sarah and I are used to dealing with."

I tell them, "Noah said jokingly Christmas this year. I just want to make sure everyone is present. My family is important to me. It is too late to have a wedding this Christmas. It is only a few weeks away."

Gabby assures me, "There is no way things will be ready that quickly. Your dress is something that cannot be rushed, and you should wait to have your wedding when you want it."

Sophia says, "I will have everything you need done for your wedding in a few weeks. You won't have to worry about the flowers." Sophia then smiles.

Ava agrees. "Everything will fall into place, and everyone will be home when you have the wedding."

Ava has her cell phone out; she is texting. I ask Sophia, "How are my wedding floral arrangements coming along?" Sophia says, "I have completed all the centerpieces but was making a few large pieces of silks, draping the head table, the gift, and cake tables. They won't take long to finish. I was thinking you would probably ask Gabby to have the wedding at the Grilling Post if you could have it on an odd day, people do it all the time if you needed to move the date sooner rather than later."

Gabby says, "Yes, we will figure it out when the guys tell us what is going on after their interviews."

Ava asks, "What time is it? The sun is out. It feels warm on my face, although the temp has not reached over thirty degrees. We should probably start back."

We all agree a four-hour ride is enough as we head back. We walk the horses around a bit to cool down from sweating after climbing the ridge of the mountain. Ava says, "I just contacted Rachel about the status of the dress, and I spoke to Sarah about the Grilling Post schedules for the next few Sundays that will be open before the New Year, just in case we need to plan a wedding."

Gabby comments, "Great! I was just going to do that! Get out of my head!"

We are all laughing again. Gabby then confirms, "I will check with the Grilling Post staff before they get to the restaurant to start their day so they can plan and be available."

Gabby conference calls them from her phone. Everyone is fine with the Sundays up until Christmas. Gabby excitedly says, "Perfect!"

We get to the barn. The horses are unsaddled as well as walked for twenty minutes by Ava and Gabby. Sophia and I work on the stalls, place grain in the trough and fresh water in their buckets. I tell Sophia, "So much for clearing my head. I may have it straightened out a bit but not cleared."

Sophia says, "You worry about the dress. We will take care of everything else."

I thank her and continue to take the wheelbarrow back around the side of the barn to the manure pile.

Dapple's New Home

I see a Dodge 3500 orange metallic truck with a matching horse trailer pull up to park at the side of the corral. It's Maggie from Deadwood, South Dakota. She enters the barn with her little girl Sky. Maggie called Mother to see if we have a meek horse she could buy to have her daughter, Sky, learn to ride. I hate parting with the old boy, but if Dapple can help someone learn to ride, he will do what he needs to make that happen. Dapple will do her no harm. A little girl will make him happy to be out riding again as we used to when I was little.

I walk over to Maggie and Sky. "Hi! So I hear you want to buy a horse to learn to ride. Dapple is such a nice horse with a wonderful disposition."

I walk them both to the stall where Dapple is eagerly waiting. "You know when I was a small girl like yourself, Dapple and I worked together for a few days until it finally happened. He is full of surprises, and I am sure he will share a few tricks with you." I look to Maggie and tell her, "I will get Dapple out and show you what I mean."

As Dapple steps out of his stall, he is a little dusty from rolling around in his sawdust I placed in the stall earlier. I tell Sky, "You will have to brush him a lot. He likes to spend time with his rider. Brushing is a time well spent with your horse."

Sky's eyes widen as I pick her up and place her on a large square crate so she may reach Dapple to brush him. "I used to use this same crate when I was your height. I was tiny like you, even smaller, when I first got Dapple from my father and mother."

I grab another brush and show her a little about grooming. Then I get the blanket and saddle I had as a little girl. I place the blanket on first then the saddle. Dapple puts his head back to watch what I am doing. I know Dapple is aware I will not be riding him since the saddle is lighter in weight, and I think he is going to like this.

I bring the horse out from the barn and into the pasture. Maggie and Sky walk along with me. "Sky, I want you to step in front of Dapple with your legs like this, then I want you to put both your arms up as if you want your mother to pick you up."

Sky walks to the front of Dapple. She extends her arms and wiggles her fingers. I am now by Sky's side. Dapple places his head between her legs and slowly lifts her up as she slides down his neck to his back. I help her flip around.

As I look at Sky, she has the biggest smile on her face. She is excited about Dapple and learning how to ride. Maggie grabs my hand and thanks me for doing this with Sky. I let Maggie know that it is just fine. "Dapple is going to love having a rider again." I explain "I did not want to put him through the extra weight of myself and a saddle. That is too much at his age."

Dapple has Sky looking like she has ridden for a long time. He is walking then trotting with Sky in the large pasture they are in to get acquainted. Maggie is asking Sky if she is ready to take her horse home. Sky, nodding her head yes and bouncing, says, "Yes."

I call Dapple to the gate. He walks briskly to exit the pasture but careful enough to not throw Sky off. Dapple knows he has a new owner. I walk in front of Dapple as he exits the fenced pasture. Maggie is amazed I do not have to lead him. I tell her, "You won't have to hold and lead, not with Dapple. He has a calm disposition about him. He always has. That is why when I heard she was a little afraid but *loves* horses, I had to talk with you. Dapple is going to love to be ridden again by a small child. He is just that type of horse."

Dapple stops at the crate, and looks back at his little rider. Sky looks at Dapple then me and asks, "What do I do?" in a quiet shy little voice.

I tell her, "How would you like to get off Dapple?"

She shrugs her little shoulders in a I-don't-know kind of way. I tell her, "What about this?" as I help her up over the horn of the Western saddle then put her back in the saddle. I tell her to try it. She then makes her way up over the horn to face backward. As she slides herself up his neck, he lowers his head slowly. She slides down his neck to his head, then he puts his head down lower so she can touch the ground, and she is off and happy. I take the saddle and blanket off of Dapple. We walk Dapple a little as I am telling her she needs to walk him until he dries off from sweat. She nods her head yes to show me she understands.

There is one more thing I want to show her with Dapple, then she can take him, and he is hers. We brush again a little, and I take Dapple back outside. I tell her to get on Dapple. She looks at me, looks at the crate, then back to me. I tell Sky to get on Dapple. She moves to the front of Dapple with her legs apart a little, and he walks to her and scoops her up gently. He lifts his head so she may slide back. She is on, and she flips herself around. She looks at me and says in a tiny voice, "I have no saddle."

I inform her, "You won't need one, although I am giving you mine and the blanket that I had when I was your age. If you want to just ride around, you won't have to be afraid. Dapple will take care of you with a saddle or bareback. He will do his part to keep you from falling and keep you safe. I want you to ride him as much as you can. You will learn from him and him you."

Sky gives Dapple a little rub with her feet to his sides and he starts walking. I open the gate, and Sky's eyes look huge. I tell her to stay calm and relax. Dapple was coming to the exit and stopped. I looked at Sky and said softly to her, "Please relax. A horse can sense when you are afraid and uneasy. He has stopped because he does not know what you want him to do. He knows you are uneasy without the saddle and just wants to do what you are not afraid of. Relax, and he will be fine."

Sky then relaxed, and Dapple walked out of the gate and walked her anywhere she wanted to go. She had Dapple all over the yard while I spoke to her mother. Sky asked, "Will Dapple do this without you being here."

"Of course, he most definitely will. Why would you think he would act any different?" I tell her with a smile, as she gets off Dapple.

Sky shrugs her shoulders again. I tell her we are going to load him up on the trailer so she may take him home. Sky smiles at her mother then looks my way and smiles at me too. She approaches me and hugs my legs. I tell her when she loads Dapple on a trailer, she should just stand to the left of the door and say, "Come, Dapple."

I walk Sky to the left back side of the trailer. Sky says, "Come, Dapple."

Dapple throws his head around a bit, whinnies, and walks right into the trailer for Sky. Sky smiles, hugs me, and thanks me. I tell her and her mother, "Dapple has a few good years left, and treated right, he will take care of you and be the best friend a girl could ever have. Remember, he loves to be brushed."

I close and latch lock the door to the back of the trailer. Dapple is talking. He seems excited to be going for a ride to his new home. Maggie hands me an envelope and tells me to take this for the horse, that she does not feel right just taking the horse. I tell her, "No, I cannot take this envelope. I am just happy for however many years Dapple has left, he will be able to bond with another child. Sky will never have another horse like him. I can tell you that."

Maggie and I smile, wave, and go our separate ways. I hear Dapple whinny then kick the side of the trailer as he leaves the ranch to find a home with a little girl who loves him. He sounds happy and excited. I was a little saddened as I make my way back to the house.

JET TO NEW YORK

I need to get my head back in the wedding. My sister should have an update on the dress. I open the door to the kitchen, and all my brothers are there with Noah and Jackson. Noah says he has the wedding plans all in order and ready to speak with me about the date. "What do you think of May 17 for the wedding date? Our invitations can be taken care of by Ava, Sophia, and Mother if you decide that is a good date," Noah exclaims.

"I looked at a few invitations with Noah but only one jumped out and made an impression on me," I exclaim.

Mother asks, "How many did you look through?"

Noah chimes in, "Too many."

I look at Noah. Noah said, "Yes. We looked at a lot. She only found one she liked."

Mother looks to me and says, "Are you satisfied with the one you thought stood out? Will you be ordering them?"

I confirm, "Yes, I could order those. They have RSVP cards with an area to circle if you would like seafood or steak and a line to request a song for the DJ to play. We can order those today. I will talk with Sarah."

Sarah has her laptop and says May 17. Sarah types in her information to order the wedding invitations and shows Noah the inside of the invitation. Sarah gets Noah's approval then has Ava, Sophia, and Gabby proofread. When everyone has done the proofreading, with the exception of me, Sarah hits send. Sarah puts in her and Joe's account information, and the invitations are now a gift from Joe and Sarah. I look at Sarah and say, "Wait, I did not look them over. What about—"

Noah chimes in, "Are you serious? You won't let me proofread our invitations? I had Rachel, Ava, Sophia, and Gabby check as well. Are you saying we are not capable of proofreading invitations? Jeez, Gabby, what did you call those particular brides?" Noah laughs and winks my way.

Gabby then says, "Bridezillas."

Noah says, "C'mon, these girls know what they are doing. One less thing you need to worry about. When the invitations arrive, the girls will mail them."

Ava, Sophia, Rachel, and Gabby say, "Yes, we will. You should not have to be bothered with that business. Let us do it. After all, we are your bridesmaids. We can handle that duty!"

Noah says, "Thank you for your help, girls. Rachel, you did not have to do that. We have money to pay for things. I have a trust."

Sarah and Joe smile and say, "We all want to take care of our little sister and her beau. Rebekah is the last one. We all helped where we could, and everyone keeps paying it forward. Now it is your and Rebekah's turn."

Noah smiled. "I am so fortunate to be a part of this family!"

I ask Rachel, "Is the dress ready?"

"Yes, the dress will be hanging in Mother's room in a few weeks. They are finishing the intricate detailing and fancy-spanshee stuff, then it will be shipped overnight to the ranch, and upon arrival, there will be a signature needed. I was thinking you and I would fly to New York, then we can do a fitting, and if it needs any resizing, they can do it, and we can refit again for the final as long as you do not get hippy or gain weight till the wedding."

"Please don't say that. Don't make me worry about weight gain. Oh my, I never thought of that!" I tell Rachel.

Rachel says, "Guess that slipped your mind. That could become a problem the day of the wedding, ya know. We will check that out tomorrow when the boys go for a horse ride. I will contact the office and see if we can fly up tomorrow. Then we can all take a quick ride in the jet before it has a new owner. We have a buyer. He did not sign papers yet, so the jet is still available."

We pack an overnight bag and then get some sleep. The alarm goes off at 5:00 a.m. We are in and out of the showers before 6:00 a.m. We say our good-byes to the guys. "See you tomorrow afternoon." We are on our way to the private hangar at the airport.

We board the jet and get seated. The jet is in line on the runway as the other planes take their turn. It is now our turn. The jet starts to take off in a high speed down the runway, and we are up and climbing. Rachel grabs us waters from the minifridge. She comes back to the seats. We are sitting around the meeting table in the middle of the jet. Rachel says, "Okay, let's breeze through the wedding business we have control of, and then we can write down what needs to be done, which should be a somewhat shorter list."

I refer to my notebook and start rattling off some things that need done. Sophia assures me, "No need to worry. The centerpieces, boutonnieres, the bridesmaids and Mother's wristlet, and your cascading wedding bouquet are all completed and are in a safe place in Mother and Father's room. They will not be disturbed until the day of the wedding." She smiles, and she can see the relief come over my face as I check that off my list.

I say, "Thank you everyone for all your help."

Sarah says, "The staff at the Grilling Post is aware of the menu and will have everything set for your wedding day."

I look to Rachel about the photographer and the cake. Rachel explains, "The pastry chef contacted Mother. Mother and the pastry chef have already decided to make five different types of cupcakes with some scones and an assortment of other pastries for the sweets table at the reception. Having cake is so overrated, and Mother wanted something different for you, something special. As for the photographer, you will definitely have a candid photo shoot for your wedding."

"So I guess there is nothing to do, nothing to worry about," I say with a big smile.

Ava then says, "What are you doing with your hair?"

"My hair. I forgot about my hair!" I say in a frightened voice. "Sarah, can we all make an appointment at your friend Lindra's salon? Can you call now and see if we can run practice styles for our hair? I have seen this beautiful messy updo with some ringlets hanging." I grab the magazine from my overnight bag and show Sarah.

Sarah says, "Yes, this can be done. I will contact Lindra to get some days scheduled. I will give her the wedding date, and we will go from there. Hold please." Sarah starts texting Lindra. "She should not take long at all. She should be texting any second now."

"When Sarah receives the text of our hair appointments, we will schedule the guys a week before the wedding so they all look handsome."

Sarah says, "Lyndra has scheduled our first two appointments to run through a few styles we would all like to try. The first appointment is Monday the sixteenth of December. The second is Saturday, the twenty-first of December. Lyndra says she can do the definite one, the morning of the wedding. Lyndra and the girls will come to the ranch to do our hair. We will use the two bathrooms on the first floor, leaving the second and third floor bathrooms for the guys."

Ava says, "It is all done. I don't believe it. All the plans for the wedding are complete."

I thank my sisters for all they have done for our wedding.

We finished tying up loose ends when we feel the jet start descending. The pilot announces we are heading into the LaGuardia Airport. Rachel says, "Here we are, girls. I even rented my old place from the new owners for the night. They rent it out until they make their permanent move to Manhattan."

The jet lands, and there is a limo awaiting our arrival. Gabby, Sophia, Sarah, and Ava cannot believe how Rachel just goes with the flow, and this is how she used to live. They comment about the lifestyles of the famous and giggle as Rachel is narrating the sights as we pass structures heading through the streets crowded with people and the important shopping department stores on the way to her old Manhattan penthouse. I am just amazed how easy it is. I know she has only been gone from New York a few months, but it is like she never left.

We arrive at Rachel's old penthouse. As the limo driver pulls up to the curb, he makes his way to the trunk of the limo and gets our bags as the door is opened by the doorman Matthew, whom I met when I stayed with Rachel several weeks ago. He puts his hand out to help each one of us out of the limo. Matthew welcomes Rachel back to New York as he says he misses Jackson and her. He gets to me and says, "Well, hello, Rebekah. It is so nice to see you again."

The girls tease me about Matthew and ask me why I did not tell them Matthew is so well put together, so handsome. I roll my eyes and say, "Yes, he is handsome—put together, as you call it. Think about it: who wants to date a doorman?"

Ava says, "Guess you are right? We all got cowboys."

Gabby says, "Since we are in town, I would like to go out for something to eat, see what it's like in the Big Apple."

Rachel says, "Okay, I got the perfect place in mind."

We get in the elevator. Ava is asking if jeans are good. Sophia is asking about dinner. Sarah is asking how long we will be out; she wants to call Joe. Gabby is anxious, and I am waiting for the elevator to stop at Rachel's old penthouse. In a few moments, the doors to the elevator open. "Wow," I say to Rachel, "this place has a country look unlike when you and

Jackson lived here. This looks more like back on the ranch."

I wander through the penthouse, looking at the interior design and furniture. Gabby, Ava, and Sophia are ready. Sarah, Rachel, and I are touching up our makeup and grabbing a bottle of water from the refrigerator. We walk to the elevator; Sophia presses the down button, and the doors open. We step into the elevator. Rachel pushes the first-floor button. We are chatting of what we would like to eat for dinner. Rachel tells us, "You may all order when we get to the establishment."

The door to the elevator opens, and Matthew is waiting to escort us to the limousine. The driver waits to open the back door to the limo; we get in, talking about what we want to eat. The driver takes us to downtown Manhattan, passing all the boutiques and shops. Rachel says, "The restaurant we want is at the end of the block."

We notice the alley blocked by beautiful large planters at either end, with tables set and canvas triangle nylon cloth strung between the buildings. Light bulbs on a strand of wire run between the overhung triangles. There are candles in small round colored bottles with wax melted down around the outside glass of the bottle. I tell the girls, "The food here is phenomenal, so delicious. The presentation of how it is placed on the plate is impeccable. It is all about the presentation, so to speak."

Sophia, Gabby, Ava, and Sarah look at me then Rachel. Rachel adds, "Rebekah loves this place! The food is delicious. She is correct."

The waiter brings the menus, and we order our drinks. Rachel fills us in on the time of the fitting with the seamstress. Rachel goes on to say, "When we get back to Wyoming, I want to stop in at the Distressed Seamstress in our town. I would like to see her work. I think I will work through her to give her more business, and this will keep my work near me, so when I speak with a client, a bride, I can be aware of the measurements and alterations to each wedding dress. Instead of using the seamstress from New York."

Ava agrees. "That would be perfect."

Our drinks come, and we order our food. Ava is chatting about her work, Sophia about the move to Texas, and Gabby states she is not worried about moving. Gabby interrupts, "Here's the food already, and Rebekah was right. The presentation is amazing. I appreciate how food comes out on a plate when I am in a restaurant. Of course, that's my business."

We eat and talk more about my wedding. I am getting tired. I am not used to being out past 8:00

p.m. We all pay our bill, leave a tip, and get to the limo. We are on our way back to the penthouse. Ava yawns. Sophia asks, "What time do we need to be ready to go to the seamstress for Rebekah's dress?"

Rachel says, "We need to arrive by 9:00 a.m. We go directly to the airport to the jet after the seamstress, please make sure you have all your belongings with you. We have no time to run back to the penthouse after the seamstress. I would not mind, but I have a virtual meeting with a client about her wedding dress. I do apologize for being so quick and sharp to everyone about our stay. We shall come to New York again when I have more time to lounge about. We will plan a girls trip and bring mother."

We are back in the penthouse, and the girls are talking about the nice dinner. We all go to our rooms to sleep for tomorrow's busy day.

We awake, ready with our overnight bag in our hand. We step into the elevator one last time. Matthew takes our bags as he opens the door to the limo and hands our bags to the limo driver. We get in, and we are on our way to the seamstress for my fitting.

Rachel informs the others to wait in the room with mirrors and stage while she helps me into my dress in the dressing room. I ask her, "Why aren't there mirrors in these rooms?"

Raven interrupts as she passes and states, "My dear Rebekah, a dressing room is not the place to see a dress in all its beauty. You will not be in a two-by-two room with 150 guests, will you? Please hurry. I have another client coming in twenty minutes, she likes to be in the shop alone."

I look to Rachel and say, "Okay, question answered." I smile and hear Raven speaking with my sisters in the other room. I add, "She sounds a little moody."

"Nah, she is being nice. We will be done soon. She always feels rushed. She is fine." Rachel says as she has me in my dress in no time. I walk to the mirrored room so Raven can check if alterations are needed. Raven says, "Everything looks good."

Raven asks me to move around in my dress to make sure I have the room and proper fit. Raven tells me to step up on the round lift to see if the length is correct. She needs to take it up an inch, then she can send the dress to the ranch. She says, "It will take about two hours, and it should be in the mail tomorrow."

I smile and tell Rachel, "This is great!"

We leave the seamstress and take the limo to the LaGuardia Airport. We are sitting in the jet reclining chairs at window seats. I am watching out the window and listening to Sophia talking to Gabby,

Rachel is chatting to me about my dress and what I think, and Ava and Sarah are sleeping. I am just watching out the window at how the ground looks so far away because we are so high in the sky, and I can see mountains for miles. In a few hours, we are landing, and we are at the ranch in no time.

We walk into the kitchen, and Gabby asks Mother and Father if they are ready to trick her parents into attending the retirement party. Our parents say they are ready. They have a plan. They are excited to pull it off. My parents ask, "How was the trip to New York, girls? How does your dress look, Rebekah?"

Ava says, "Rebekah looks stunning, so beautiful in her dress. I cannot believe she thought of the dress when she was a child. That's amazing."

Rachel says, "I added some intricate detail and some other things. When we were kids, I just sketched a dress. I added the fancy glitz—with her permission, of course—just recently. We never thought of fancy glitz when we were kids. Just the plain dress is what excited us."

Rachel smiles and hugs me.

PARTY TIME

My parents' ranch hands have been working the ranch since the cattle are in the barn until the spring. The cattle are fed hay and proteins, along with some grains. There are only three hands normally, six to eight stay or commute back and forth to the ranch. There is a bunkhouse in the barn with a kitchen, sitting room with television, heat, and of course, a full bathroom.

Our parents have spoken to the ranch hands in regard to being available more now that their boys are going their separate ways since college is completed and expectations of careers await them. Our parents informed the ranch hands Joe, Jackson, and Noah are also available to help out on the weekends so the others may go home to their families then come to the ranch during the week.

Mother and Father come back from the barn. They are mentioning the ranch hands, and their families should be asked to celebrate Christmas with our family since some of their children are in the other states with other commitments. My parents know it is hard for some not to have their loved ones with them during the holidays, so they will suggest Christmas dinner with our family.

It is Sunday morning, the morning of the retirement/going-away party. The house has been busy early since we have so much going on today. They are getting ready for church dressing a little fancier for the after church event. Mother texts Gabby's parents to confirm they are still on for later today.

Good Morning Bella & Logan

Just dropping you a quick line to make sure we are still on for later today. Can't wait to get together with you both. This is going to be a wonderful overdue time since everyone is always so busy. Text as soon as you get this as we will be over after church to pick you up.

Abigail

Mother turns her phone on silent to make sure she has no loud noises during the sermon.

Our family arrives at church. As we make our way up the steps to the foyer of the church, Mother sees Bella and Logan, Gabby's parents, just inside the door, waiting to sit with them. Gabby sees them right away and is so excited. We all are smiling as we say good morning to the pastor, who greets everyone as they come into the church.

As Noah approaches Pastor Rob, he tells Pastor Rob, "Things are moving pretty quickly. May I speak to you after church? We are looking at May 17." Noah gives a wink.

Pastor Rob shakes Noah's hand as he nods yes and says, "Good morning, Noah!" with a smile and a wink back.

Noah smiles and follows me to the pew.

The pastor closes the doors to the church, and with the church bells ringing the most beautiful sound, the pastor makes his way to the front of the church. The pastor starts out by welcoming everyone and then proceeds to tell a story about communication, trust, and love for each other and others.

After an hour, we sing a song or two, say a prayer, and the bells ring again as the pastor makes his way back to the doors of the church to shake hands, to tell everyone to have a great day. Noah and I wait until last, letting everyone go ahead of us. Noah said, "I enjoyed the sermon this morning."

Pastor Rob, with his hand on Noah's shoulder, says, "I thought since you told me at the door things are happening in May"—as he says this, he winks and smiles—"I would not only speak to you and Rebekah but everyone about the three most important things in a marriage. Every now and again, everyone needs a reminder as to what makes a marriage work, and everyone got a refresher or a little reminder, as I like to call it. Doesn't hurt to throw reminders in every now and again. Sermons are to learn from, and I'm glad you enjoyed it."

Noah quickly says, "I actually got the family I never had with Rebekah's family." Noah proceeds to reflect briefly on his life growing up. Pastor Rob anxiously says, "I cannot wait to meet Fran and her family at your wedding. They sound like wonderful caring people."

Pastor Rob hugs me and states, "I think you kids are going to be just fine. You let me know where. I do not want to be late, and I need to definitely be there. I have married all the Sawyer children to their spouses. It just would not be right if I did not show up for the last child to marry her beau. No, no, just would not be right. What is the date so I can mark my schedule?"

Noah says eagerly, "May 17."

Pastor Rob says, "Thank you. See you next week. Have a great Sunday!"

Noah asks if there is something else they need to do with the pastor. Pastor Rob says, "Nah, nothing I can think of. I think you have told me everything I need to know."

They say their goodbyes and head to the Suburban, where my brothers and sister with their spouses are waiting. We head to the Grilling Post for the retirement party.

Noah lent Mother and Father his Jeep. The family is chatting about the party and is excited about helping Gabby make this the best party ever. Gabby is hopeful the staff will be able to spend time with her parents, their boss. The family tells her, "We will chip in where we can so the staff will be able to have a great time as well."

The siblings arrive at the Grilling Post to find Avery and Ashton parking cars in the back lot so Gabby's parents won't know there is anything going on. Avery and Ashton are Allianna's two older boys. Gabby says, "I commend Allianna. I never thought of that!"

Gabby stops to speak to the boys and thanks them. They both smile, nodding their heads yes and assuring the guests are all here. Avery says, "We were told Joe and Abigail will be bringing your parents."

Gabby says, "That is correct."

Ashton then assures her, "Everyone is here! We will leave. Thank you for letting us help. This was the most fun we've had in a while. We enjoyed talking, welcoming the guests, and parking their cars. This did not seem like work at all. We will be back in two hours to see if anyone will be leaving. We will wait to make sure everyone has their cars as they leave the party. We pretty much know which car belongs to each guest. See you in two hours."

Gabby thanks them and says, "See you later."

Gabby was sideswiped by the valet parking but thinks she may make this part of the restaurant. Gabby is thinking so as to not forget to tell Allianna thank you and to see if those boys would like a job parking cars for the Grilling Post during working hours.

We enter and say our hellos before her parents arrive. Gabby grabs the mic from the DJ to say a few words to everyone. "Good evening! My parents should be here any second now. If you could just stay a little quiet so they don't hear everyone when they come in, that would be great!"

Gabby joins the rest of the family to await the arrival of her parents. Sarah comes from the kitchen, checking on the staff. "Everyone is doing just fine, and the staff worked it out that they can join us for dinner."

Ava receives a text that they have arrived! Gabby runs to the DJ, grabs the mic, and states, "My parents are in the parking lot."

The lights go dim; everyone is quiet. I hear the chef tell the kitchen staff not to make too much noise. Gabby hears the door to the restaurant lobby open, our parents chatting with each other. As they open the door to the dining area, everyone yells, "Surprise!"

Bella and Logan have the most surprised look on their faces. They are working their way through the crowd, saying their hellos and glad they all came to the surprise shindig. Gabby takes the mic from the DJ, "We would like to thank you for coming to the retirement going-away party for my parents. The food will be on the buffet soon, and then you can file through. There is a small bar with microbrewed beers, two mixers, and two kinds of wine to the right of the buffet. There is a glass of champagne sitting at your place on the table. If everyone would raise their glass to toast the new chapter of my parents' life."

Everyone lifts their glasses and toasts. Gabby then says, "Our valet parking attendants will be returning in two hours to retrieve cars of guests that plan on leaving early. For now, enjoy the evening." She hands the mic back to the DJ as the dinner music restarts.

The wait staff finishes placing the food on the buffet. Allianna walks across the room to have Gabby's parents start the line. Jacob, his brothers, and his sisters make their way through the line with their spouses after Logan and Bella. They all sit between other guests so they can clean off tables and load the dishwasher when the time comes. Chef Shay and the kitchen staff come out and go through the line. Everyone is finally seated, and the grazing table has been unveiled by the wait staff.

Dinner was delicious. The guests compliment the chef and wait staff for such a lovely dinner and a perfect start to a wonderful evening. Everyone is enjoying themselves. Gabby and the family are clearing the tables, rinsing the dishes, and placing them in the dishwasher. The guests are relaxing and enjoying the rest of the evening, talking, drinking, and dancing with each other.

I see there are a few guests leaving. Gabby's parents are by the door, saying their goodbyes to the older guests who are heading out to the parking lot. Gabby hurries outside to get some night air. Ashton and Avery are getting the cars for the guests who are leaving, helping them in and wishing them a good night.

After the boys get the last of the cars of the guests who are on their way out early, Gabby calls the young fellows to the patio area of the Grilling Post. She wants to ask them a question. "I am guessing you are seventeen or eighteen years of age, if not older, is that correct to say?"

The boys nod their heads and say, "Yes, seventeen and eighteen years old."

"I want to speak with you first because you are doing such a swell job. How would you like a full-time job parking approximately one hundred to 165 cars a night? I will have to check into what I would do to go about having this perk for our guests at the Grilling Post. Would you two be interested? I am asking before I ask your mother, Allianna. What do you say?"

The boys look at each other and say, "There is no valet parking at the Grilling Post."

I inform them, "There is if I say there is. I will speak to your mother. Are you two interested?"

They both say, "Yes, we would love this job. It does not feel like a job at all."

Gabby tells them, "I will speak with your mother tonight after the party so she has time to think about it. I need to find out what type of insurance I will need to have the two of you park cars. Then I can tell you how much I can give you as pay as well. I cannot offer a pay amount without checking things on my end, then I can get back to you."

The boys are excited about their first job. "Sure thing," they say with a smile. "Let us know when to start."

Gabby tells them, "You will be hearing from me in about a week."

She walks back into the party and her family. She sees Allianna across the room, chatting with her parents and figures she will text her tomorrow about the job for Ashton and Avery at the Grilling Post.

DJ Jazzy has everyone on the dance floor doing the line dance to an oldie. Abigail, Joe, Bella, and Logan are having a great time. They have been on the floor, dancing all night, with the exception of when guests are leaving.

Gabby sits at a table in the back of the room. Gabby is a little antsy and wonders how the kitchen is doing. She walks through the doors. The dishwasher is finished, and Noah and I are putting the dishes away. "We are almost done."

Joe and Jacob are lifting the heavy pots so the girls can stick them in the dishwasher now that the dishes are away. Ava and Sophia are wrapping the dry utensils in the linen napkins. Sarah and Rachel finish placing the pots in the dishwasher and move to cleaning the counters. Gabby says, "Wow, the kitchen looks great! Make sure you put the rest of the leftover meat in to-go containers to take home to the ranch for dinner tomorrow. I will take some out to my parents so they can snack tomorrow before their drive to Arizona."

We all leave the kitchen, the ovens off, food away, dishes cleaned, utensils wrapped. The guys finish sweeping and mopping the kitchen floor. That only took an hour and a half—not bad. The family goes back to the party.

Gabby sees the wait staff enter the kitchen and in a few moments come back out with smiles on their faces, talking among themselves about how everything has been cleaned up in the kitchen. Gabby took the liberty of taking the tablecloths off the tables that are empty as well as the food tables. She hands them to Sarah to throw in the washing machine through the door labeled "Utility Room Employees Only."

DJ Jazzy has everyone doing a slow dance. Ava says to Gabby, "I think your parents enjoyed themselves. They were able to see all the guests that were here and some they spent hours with."

"Speaking of hours," Gabby says, "probably soon time to call it a night. I will head back into the office to get the envelopes to pay the help, and then we can do last call for our tiny makeshift bar and go home to relax. We have been here for six hours. Whatever is left to do, the kitchen and wait staff can do."

Jacob says, "I will go with you to the office, then we will leave."

DJ Jazzy notifies the remaining guests of last call for alcohol at the minibar. Avery and Ashton bring the last of the cars around. After the guests are all gone and everyone is paid, Gabby calls to Avery and Ashton. They come to the foyer of the Grilling Post. Gabby hands them an envelope and tells them everyone gets paid tonight. Smiles come across their faces as they reach out and take the envelopes. Jacob and Gabby say thank you and goodnight as the staff are cleaning up the snack table.

Gabby, Jacob, Joe, Abigail, and all the family walk Logan and Bella to the suburban. We tell them we will visit sometime. They are thrilled and can't wait to see everyone again. They get in the suburban so Joe and Abigail can drive them to the church lot to get their SUV. Jacob hands them the platters, hugs them, and wishes them well on their trip. Jacob turns to the rest of the family, puts his arm around Gabby, and states, "Now there's a wedding to get ready for!"

Sarah says, "Yes. Before we start talking about the wedding, I have some news since we are all together. You all know I went to the doctor the other day. I am…correction: Joe and I—we are having identical twin girls."

Joe says, "Another secret!"

Sarah says, "No, another surprise."

Everyone is congratulating Joe and Sarah.

Mother says, "Let's get back to the house so we can have a coffee. Sounds like we have more to talk about.

A BOY OR A GIRL?

We arrive at the ranch and meet in the kitchen. Father starts a pot of coffee. Mother is placing cupcakes she wants us to sample on a tray in the center of the kitchen bar. She has five different kinds. She tells us, "These are the flavors for Noah and Rebekah's wedding. Let me know please what your thoughts are about my selection." Ava and Sophia grab the cups, and Rachel is pouring the coffee. Father is getting ready to brew another pot.

Father asks what names they thought of for the girls. "I know you think it may be too early to be thinking of names, but these things creep up on you, and before you know it, you will need to throw names out there, names that are fitting for not only you as parents but also the children. They should have strong names, names that will hold them all through their lives. What I mean is names people will take seriously."

Joe and Sarah agreed. "We thought about that. Names that are bold and strong yet feminine at the same time."

Father said, "You got it!"

Joe said, "Our daughters' names will be Palmer Abigail and Harper Grace. These are the names we picked last night."

Sarah is smiling, waiting to hear the response to the names. Father is nodding his head; Mother is agreeing these names are beautiful names. "Palmer and Harper," Mother and Father say. "We love those names."

Everyone agrees and looks to Jackson and Rachel to see if she found anything out at her visit since they are around the same due date. Rachel states, "You will all have to wait. I am not ruining Joe and Sarah's thunder. No way!"

Rachel says, "That's not happening. I will deliver our news after I tell Jackson."

Jackson looks at Rachel and smiles. He grabs Rachel by the hand and takes her to the third floor. Everyone is running after them, leaving Mother and Father in the kitchen. Father yells to us, "Find out and bring the news back to the kitchen please!"

All are gathered on the stairs outside the third-floor penthouse. Jeremiah reaches in his pocket and pulls out this long, slender piece of metal with a hook on the end. He reaches up and slides it quietly into the hole in the doorknob; it clicks, then he slowly and quietly turns the knob and tells us in a whisper, "When the door starts to open, just run in because the door squeaks."

The door is opened quickly, and we rush in like a football team running onto the playing field. We see Jackson and Rachel sitting on the chest at the end of Jeremiah's bed. We all gather around and ask what Jackson was told. We know Rachel is a steel trap! Rachel and Sarah are the same when it comes to secrets. Jackson says, "We are having a little boy," as tears run down his face. "His name will be Jackson Sebastian or Sebastian Jackson."

Rachel is shaking her head and says, "The doc in New York told me stress and things would make this a difficult pregnancy. I was told the wrong time frame I am to have our child, by a few weeks after Sarah. I did not want anyone to know that right away, so I kept it between Jackson and me. There was a possibility of only having one child as well, which is great too. I am not as talented as Mother was having all of us, so I am glad I am only having one. I would like to ease into parenting."

The family comes back to the kitchen to tell Mother and Father they will have to wait for Jackson and Rachel to tell them. Jackson and Rachel are summoned to the kitchen by Mother, laughing and telling them to give them the news. Our parents are happy for all and say any grandchildren they get to spoil in the years to come will be a blessing.

Noah and I make our way to the living room. Noah says, "Your family has so much fun with everyone's news and happenings. I love being a part of this large family."

Noah tells me that he will be relieving the ranch hands for the next couple of days so they can spend time with their families. I say, "Okay, that's fine."

Noah says, "Just to feed and make sure the pregnant cattle are taken care of. The one is due to have a calf any day now."

They are chatting about our wedding to make sure they have everything covered. Jeremiah comes in and hands us ten cupcakes and tells us to get tasting. "Oh my!" Noah says. "What in the world? Do all of you like them?"

Noah and I make our way back into the kitchen. Noah and I grab a cupcake and start to taste them. We share and taste, and we like them all. Mother is happy and tells everyone these are the flavors we are having for the reception—no cake but cupcakes in a large tier arrangement with an assortment of pastries on the round table graced with silk swags draped to the front to set the cupcake table off with some twinkle lights spread throughout.

I ask my brothers to make sure they will be present for the wedding, and they assure me they will be there; they would not miss it. Rachel reminds them to go to their fitting tomorrow at the Tall Pines Tuxedo Shop. They all shake their heads and wave their hands in the air. Noah states, "We will need to be at Tall Pines Tuxedo Shop by 10:00 a.m. Our appointment is 10:00 a.m. to 12:00 p.m. to order and reserve the tux and tails to shoes and socks."

My brothers roll their eyes and chuckle with a smirky smile, as if I am not to worry. They tell me to not get my petticoat in a bunch. As they are leaving the kitchen, they tell me, "We have been hearing this for the past week. We know."

I informed them with a shout out the kitchen door as they walked across the yard to the barn, "I am a nervous bride. Humor me."

They yell, "We love you, Rebekah!" They turn to smile to me, and they walk through the door of the barn as it closes behind them.

ON THEIR WAY

It's the end of the week. Gabby drove Jacob to the airport. Gabby said it was hard saying goodbye. She hopes this job opportunity is everything he thinks it is and more. She wants this to be the one for him. He talked about this position since before he applied for the job. She just hopes he is not disappointed or has a bad experience that may show him this is not the position for him. She cried all the way home from the airport. She knows he will be home at the end of next week but misses him dearly.

Gabby texts Mother,

> Jacob will call once he gets to the hotel and is settled. It was hard to leave him even though he will return next Friday evening. I will notify you when I hear from him.

I miss him so much and he is only gone a few minutes.

Love you,
Gabby

Mother has another text message alert. It's Sophia.

Jeremiah just boarded a flight to Texas. I miss him already and he only left a few minutes ago. I am walking out of the airport. I will be on my way home in a few moments. I am going to miss everyone when I have to go with Jeremiah. I have been crying since before he left. I know he had to go but I cannot stand to be without him. May I stay over until his return? I will stop at the house to grab clothes and be over. I will not be able to stay in our home without him.

See you soon. Love, Sophia

Mother talks to Father about Sophia's text message. Mother then goes on to say, "Gabby will probably be over too. Those girls miss the boys, and they just left. They are going to be so lonely. It will be the longest week of their lives. Sophia is grabbing some clothes and personal things, and she will be here to stay until Jeremiah returns."

Father says, "You better text Gabby and tell her to grab some things from their home and come over as well. They are used to having the boys home. Tell them to come and stay. I would rather have them here so they have someone to talk to, than stay in an empty house, thinking about my sons not being there."

Father sits in his chair, turns the light on, reaches for the newspaper as he presses the news channel on the remote for the flat screen above the fireplace. "After the news, I need to get out to the barn. I am working on a little something for Rachel and Sarah for Christmas," Father states.

Mother texts Gabby,

> Gabby we would like if you would come to the main house and stay until Jacob returns at the end of next week. Sophia is going

to stop by her home to grab some things and spend the week with us. We think you should as well. We will be expecting you.

See you soon, Mother

Mother presses send.

Mother tells Father, "The girls should be here soon."

Father looks over his paper and smiles "Good."

After two hours go by, Gabby texts mother,

Just wanted you to know Jacob arrived at the airport and he is on his way to the hotel. Then he said he will be grabbing a bite to eat and run by his future employers' site to make sure he knows where he is going tomorrow. He said he will contact me every night he gets back from his days at the lab.

I am grabbing a few of my personal things and I will be over soon. I will bring the horse since I won't be back until Jacob gets back. It is not snowing yet but I see the weathermen are calling for snow in a few days. A storm of all things.

I really wish Jacob was home. See you soon.

Love you
Gabby

Mother texts back,

See you soon! Be careful!

Love you,
Mother

Mother presses send. She is reading the text message from Sophia.

I spoke to Gabby and I will be bringing my horse over to the barn while I stay. There is a storm coming soon and I feel it best to ride her over so I do not have to try to get to our home to feed her. I am actually on my way. I'm just coming around the meadow by the lake.

I spoke to Jeremiah. I will tell you all about that when I get there.

See you soon.

Sophia

Mother replies,

Ok, see you soon. Be careful!

I can't wait to hear of the call from Jeremiah.

Love you
Mother

Mother presses send.

The girls arrive and place their horses in the barn. Mother sees the girls coming across the snow-covered yard, carrying their bags to the house. They come in through the kitchen and take their things to the third floor. Sophia yells to Mother as she is climbing the stairs, "I will be right back to tell you about Jeremiah's phone call!"

Sophia hurries back to the kitchen. Mother has caramel coffee sitting on the kitchen bar for Sophia and Gabby as she waits eagerly to hear about Jeremiah's phone call. Sophia sits across from Mother and starts to tell her of the phone call, Sophia states, "The professor of cardiology picked him up at the airport and took him to the hotel to drop off his things. He told me the hospital and hotel are next to each other, within walking distance, which he is very happy about. He was on his way to dinner with the professor when he called me.

"Jeremiah sounded real excited. He said the neighborhood surrounding the hospital is beautiful as well, and he could see us living there for a few years till he was done with his residency. I told him not to be so blinded by the material things he can see. He needs to decide on the program first, not the neighborhood. I know he was just trying to make me feel excited. He told me he would contact me every night around 9:00 p.m.

"I did tell Jeremiah I am staying with you and Father, that I missed him when he walked on that plane. I felt I could not stand to be away from him even though he just left. Jeremiah is happy I am staying so I would not be alone. He told me he would see me in a week."

Mother admits, "Sounds like he is excited to be there. How impressive, the professor of cardiology picking him up at the airport and taking him to dinner, showing him around the neighborhood. That is a very hospitable gesture. I am thinking it is a little too early to show Jeremiah around the area unless, like Jeremiah said, the neighborhood is on the way to the hospital. Possibly they are just anxious and excited, which is great as well. Can't wait to hear how the entire visit goes."

Father comes to the kitchen, and Sophia and Mother tell Father about the phone call. Father states, "I cannot wait to have both boys back home to see what they decide."

Jacob and Jeremiah called the girls every night. The girls were so happy. The phone calls were the comfort they needed to make it through their time apart.

BIDDING WAR BEGINS

Ava calls several contractors to get estimates on the summer kitchen renovations. Joshua meets with three this afternoon, and Ava meets with four later in the day. Ava does a walk-through of the summer kitchen with the contractors then takes them to the kitchen of the main house to meet with Joshua to look over plans. Ava and Joshua continue this until the seventh contractor completes both the walk-through and the viewing of the plans. Ava shakes their hands and tells them to get an estimate together and drop it at the secure business box at the gate to the ranch labeled "AJ Architecture." The estimates will be in the box in five or less days, per the contractors.

Ava asked that they also include a few references. "We would like to see the completed work you have done so we can help Jackson and Rachel make a decision." Ava and Joshua thank the contractors for their time, shake hands, and say their goodbyes.

Joshua and Ava take a minute to regroup in the living room. They tell Father they are staying the night since they are exhausted. Mother asks when the contractors will be starting. Ava said, "At the latest, a month from now, and at the earliest, Monday two weeks from now. We will be speaking to Jackson and Rachel as soon as we have all the estimates for them to review. There will be some estimates that are cheap, some expensive, and some middle of the road. The question is what their work is like, or what is the quality of the job being performed? That is where the references come in handy. We could recommend the contractors for future projects as well.

"All the contractors that came were very reputable, according to the Internet. We will help go through the estimates and references with Rachel and Jackson, then the remodeling will begin. Rachel and Jackson can hire two or three of the contractors so they can get the summer kitchen done quicker or work with one contractor. We will chat in a few days with Rachel and Jackson.

"Of course, with all this snow we keep getting, they may be able to work on the basement and the kitchen but have to wait for spring thaw to work on the additions needed. Not in any rush because I think picking a contractor is like picking a husband. You need someone who is dependable, work ethic is precise, and he is someone you can trust."

Mother says, "Ava, what a great way to think. I would have never thought of comparing a contractor to a husband. You are absolutely correct. I agree. I sure do."

CHRISTMAS AND CALVING

Jeremiah and Jacob will be back a few days before Christmas. The girls will be busy with Christmas and should not have much time to miss them. Mother wants to make a store list. I write everything she rattles off while she runs around the kitchen, checking the cabinets for ingredients. Mother, thinking out loud, says, "Sarah is making cranberry sauce. I will need the ingredients," as she continues with the list within her mind.

"Sophia is making the garlic sour cream mashed potatoes and also the gravies and sauces for the beef and seafood dishes."

Mother flips through the Rolodex in her mind, telling me everything we need. "Ava is making crab cakes. Please add real lump crab to the list, about three pounds."

Gabby kicks in to add more to my list from her thoughts. "I will be making some multigrain honey-buttered knot bread with some seasoned sides."

Mother says, "Rebekah and I will be running to the market to grab the groceries now that she has it all written. We also need to add our cookie ingredients. I will grab the paper with the list of cookies I printed from the Internet."

"I can't wait!" Gabby chimes in.

Sarah says, "Have you forgotten already, Mother? I have the grocery list covered when you are done adding to it."

Mother looks it over and hands it to Sarah. "You do remember I made an account for you online before Thanksgiving, right?"

Mother says, "Oh, that's right! I will let you know when the list is complete. Thank you! I forgot, although I like to walk through the grocery store with the exception of holidays. I need to remember I can have you enter it on the computer under our account for the grocery store to have it delivered. Sarah, they do deliver, don't they?"

Sarah looks at Mother and nods her head yes, saying, "Most definitely."

"Perfect! That will give me more time to do other things." Mother looks at us with a smile and says, "Well, you know what to do."

Everyone heads to the rooms they need to clean. Mother likes to do a light house clean before the holidays. We clean the windows and sill throughout the house as well as the baseboard around the bottom of all the rooms. We dust, wax, and polish from the ceiling fans to the floors. Ava and I are busy on the ladder cleaning fan blades. Sarah and Mother collect the bed clothes to wash, and Gabby and Sophia hang the blankets on the veranda railing on the first and second story. We all pitch in and scrub the bathrooms. In four hours, we meet in the kitchen for a light lunch.

I am smelling ziti, or is it Italian bread? Could be both. Mother must have prepared a pan and placed it in the oven earlier this morning. I pull on the oven door; there are two large pans of ziti with the smell of a garlic cheese bread. I pull on the other oven door. My mouth is watering; my stomach is growling.

Noah enters the kitchen from the barn; he is asking mother for old sheets. Mother goes to the closet under the stairs. She hands him a handful of sheets. She then asks, "How many?"

Noah states, "Five so far. They are all standing and drinking from their mothers. We just want to be ready for the other ten mothers. Not sure when they are coming. Father told us it is possible over the next few days, maybe a week, unknown, but we should have more soon."

Mother smiles and says, "When you hear the dinner bell, send someone to the kitchen to grab you boys a pan of ziti and garlic cheese bread."

Noah smiles. "Thank you for the sheets." He is rushing to get back out to the barn.

"Sure thing!" Mother replies.

Noah is off to the barn. We finish up our lunch, place the dishes in the dishwasher, and go back to cleaning. We are all downstairs. Ava says, "It's been five days since we spoke to the contractors. I need to run to the secure box at the end of the driveway to check on it when we take another break."

Mother says, "Let's ask the guys to hook up the sleigh, and we will take a ride. You should have contractors' estimates by now, don't you think? Rebekah, could you run out to the guys to ask if they can hook Duchess to the sleigh?"

As I run from the kitchen, I'm stepping into my winter boots. I yell, "I'm on it!" I grab my warm jacket by the door. Across the porch, down the stairs to the snow-covered ground, and I am almost at the barn. As I enter the barn, I hear the guys are busy delivering another calf, and I hear Jackson say, "I cannot believe this one has two. That's amazing!"

Noah is carrying the warm bucket of water to clean off the calf. Then he helps it stand, and it wobbles to its mother to drink.

I see the most amazing thing happening in the barn. The calves that were born earlier have taken to their mothers to drink and lay with their mothers to stay warm. Noah asks, "Did you need something?"

I tell Noah, "I am hooking Duchess up to the sleigh. Mother told me we are taking a ride to the end of the driveway to check the security strong box for the estimates the contractors were to have for Ava and Joshua."

My brother Joe hears me and says, "I will help Rebekah, and I will return for the next one since we are still waiting for the calf to be born."

While Joe is helping me hook Duchess to the sleigh, I tell Joe, "Dinner will be ready soon. Mother said it should be pretty close to ready when we get back from our ride. Then we will bring it to the barn for everyone to eat."

Joe finished hooking the sleigh to Duchess. He tells me he will notify the rest, and I am off to pick up everyone at the house. I see them on the porch. They heard Duchess' bells ringing as we pulled out of the barn. Mother holds two large blankets, and a hot chocolate for me. The rest are holding tight to their coffees.

I pull close to the house and everyone is on the sleigh. Mother throws the other blanket up front to Rachel, Ava, and me. This is so nice. Everyone is talking about what they bought the guys for Christmas. Ava mentions there is a large package for Mother at their home. It came a week ago. Mother laughs and states she has no idea what it could possibly be. Mother tells us what she got Father, not that Father needs anything. It is coming on Christmas. Ava, Sophia, Gabby, and Rachel tell us they have surprises for Christmas for the guys as well.

Christmas is always a great time of year for our family. Just getting together is enough. We really don't need the surprise of gifts, but the girls all agree they will take whatever the guys give them. They giggle. Gabby says, "We have the gifts for our husbands in the office at the Grilling Post locked up in the safe, of course."

"The boys won't be snooping anytime soon."

Ava is wondering, "Out of the seven that came to give estimates, I wonder how many contractors will submit estimates. I think there are two we won't hear from. I got the feeling by the way they were talking that this is not a large enough job for them. I hope they prove me wrong!"

Ava jumps from the sleigh and checks the box. She shuffles a handful of large manila envelopes to get some order, approaches the sleigh, reaches up to grab the rail, steps up with a smile, and says, "I hold in my hand six of seven contractor estimates. Joshua will be so pleased."

Mother says, "Time will tell. The other contractor has a few days until his time is up."

Ava adds, "The contractor is either taking advantage of the time that is left to have a precise estimate, or they are procrastinating and hopeful their estimates fall into the perfect numbers to get them the job. There is no room for procrastinators. Those types don't put the quality and time into their work. I am hoping the last one has a well-thought-out estimate. This may make that one the better of the six I already have."

When we get back to the house, Ava opens the envelopes to see what the estimate cost will be from each contractor. "They are around the same price. Not bad. I will speak with Joshua and see what his thoughts are in regards to these numbers. It is possible Joshua may want to make sure these are solid estimates. I wonder if we should get estimates from other contractors. I think these estimates are pretty reasonable. I will show Joshua when he comes in from the barn." Ava places the envelopes on the kitchen counter and goes back outside.

Mother tells Ava to climb back onto the sleigh. Mother walks swiftly but carefully into the house to grab the hot stoneware from the oven. She then hands the food to Sarah as she gets back on the sleigh. She tells us to take her to the barn. She wants to check on the guys and give them the cheesy garlic bread and ziti.

When we get to the barn, I jump down then put my hands out to grab the warm stoneware of ziti from Sarah. I hand the ziti back to Mother. My other sisters climb down off the sleigh and make their way to the glow of light in the bottom of the barn.

As we get closer, we smell freshly brewed coffee with a hint of caramel. I hear Father speaking to Noah as he pours him a cup of coffee. We chat with the guys a bit while Mother puts the food on the table in the other room. Joshua says, "We are just waiting around like fathers in a maternity ward."

The guys laugh and kid around as to which calf looks like them, pointing out different characteristics. Father grabs a chair and says he likes hanging out with the boys and his new addition, Noah. I reach out and take Noah's hand. I smile at him and tell him he is a part of a big family. Father then goes on to say Noah may be helping on the ranch instead of continuing college. I look at Noah, and he smiles. Noah tells me, "Hanging out in the barn is amazing. I enjoy bonding with your brothers and father, not to mention the birth of all the newborn calves. Life is just astounding to watch and helping the heifers with their calves."

Mother smiles. "Our pan should be done, and we can eat as well. Don't rush, girls. Take your time to visit with the guys and the new additions to our livestock."

Gabby tells Mother, "Wait, I will walk along with you to the house."

The girls hang out with the new calves for a bit, then Sarah mentions she is starving, smelling the ziti Mother brought to the barn for the guys. I agree. "Yes, we should all head back to the house to eat."

Sarah, Ava, Sophia, and I say our good nights to our guys. We tell them, "We will be back out to the barn to check on the baby calves tomorrow."

Noah reaches out to me, hugs me tight, and tells me, "I will be staying in the bunkhouse in the barn with the rest until we know the mothers are done giving birth."

I tell him, "That is fine. Watching our calves be born is more important right now than anything."

Noah smiles, kisses me on my forehead, and wishes me sweet dreams. I say, "Back at cha!" as I smooch him on his cheek. We smile at each other, and I am on my way to the house with my sisters.

Mother has the ziti and garlic cheese bread on the dining room table. Sarah says the prayer, thanking the good Lord for our family, food, and new little additions in the barn. The topic is Christmas Eve and Christmas Day. Sarah reassures Mother the groceries will be arriving tomorrow morning, 9:00 a.m. sharp. Mother is pleased.

DECEMBER 23

I hear a vehicle pull up to the house. I looked out the bedroom window to see our grocery delivery is here. I cannot believe how much food Mother ordered. Mother is rustling around downstairs. The three young boys from the market are hustling the many brown paper bags of groceries in the house. I hear Mother thank the boys for carrying the groceries to the kitchen. The boys say how busy they are this morning. Mother hands them a little zippy bag of homemade cookies with a to-go cup of hot chocolate. She wishes them a Merry Christmas and Happy New Year as they get back into the delivery truck. Off they go, blowing their horn out our driveway.

I lay back in my bed, my eyes closed, trying to relax, but I can't. Today is the day before Christmas Eve. The boys should be home sometime today. I look forward to the time when my nieces and nephew celebrate the Christmas holiday. Just to see their faces light up, the twinkle in their eyes, the magic of Christmas will once again fill this house as it did when my brothers, sister, and I were just small children.

I hear someone coming up the stairs. It's Noah. Noah says he has to speak with me about college. I sit on the edge of the bed. I tell him, "Okay, I am all ears!"

I look at him with a smile. I notice he has a worried look on his face and a hesitation in his voice. I ask him if there is something wrong. He starts out by saying, "I enjoy the ranch and think I would like to help Joe run the ranch instead of going back to school." Noah looks at me. "If you feel strongly about us going to college together—"

I stop him. "No, things are finally coming together for us. We are engaged, we have a wedding date. I saw the look on my father's face when he mentioned you helping out when I was in the barn last night. I think it would be great! College is only two months for me. I'm commuting. I will be taking care of the books at the ranch." Rambling on, I stop. "Did you talk with Joe?"

"Actually," Noah says, "both Joe and your father approached me. Joe and I have covered a lot of ground between delivering calves and doing other chores while we spent those many days in the barn. I would love to be included in the family business. I have degrees. I have knowledge to fall back on if this does not work out, but I am sure this will, and I can use my degrees to help out if I need to, but I like the feel of the hard-work labor. This is my family now."

He picks me up, swings me around as if I were a child. "Do you know how happy I am?"

I ask, "Are you marrying my family, or do you love me?"

Noah says that he loves both. He would do anything for me and my family.

I add, "I should have never questioned that. I am sorry. My plan is to hang a shingle to do taxes. I will see about a small space in town. I could place a secure box on the building by the front door for customers to place their information in an envelope and drop it off after hours. Business taxes usually are done throughout the year quarterly. I want to do that also. I was thinking of dabbling in real estate, but I am not absolutely positive."

"Sounds like a great idea! Now about the wedding," Noah replies, "how are the details coming along? I want to sit with you and hear all that's been decided since we last spoke." He smiles. "I must get back to the barn to help clean up. All the mothers are done having their calves for now."

I look at Noah. Noah then looks at me and tells me he can't wait until our wedding in May. He says, "I think about our wedding day all the time. I cannot get you out of my mind."

I hug Noah and thank him for being able to talk to me about anything. "Honest communication is important in a relationship, at least it is to me, and it is good for us," I tell Noah.

We make our way to the stairs as Father and the rest come in through the kitchen from the barn. The girls want to give Mother and Father their gifts early. "Jacob and Jeremiah are going to be attending virtually on the flat screen, so everyone will be here, one way or another. The boys are excited to give Mother and Father their gifts too, so we all decided to do it this way," Sarah states.

We all rush to the living room. The boys are on the flat screen above the fireplace. They both wish everyone a Merry Christmas. Father states, "I hope this is not how Christmases are going to be in the future," as he chuckles. "Better than not seeing the boys at all, though."

Jeremiah and Jacob tell the girls, "Give Mother and Father their gift."

The girls present Mother and Father with a large white envelope. Father tells Mother, "You can open this. I will wait to see and help if you need it."

Mother opens the envelope and starts to cry. "This is a trip for three months of travel across the United States, including Hawaii and Alaska, to see all the beauties of our great nation and to spend time with the differences of culture, climate, and relaxation in the USA, then to continue to fly internationally to Ireland and Greece."

Mother and Father are excited. "We have not had time away from the ranch since before you were born. The only trip we would take is to the grocery store, feed mill, and possibly deliver cattle to a drop-off point in the next surrounding state."

Mother and Father thank us for thinking of them. The boys say they will be home to help take care of the ranch before they leave on their business adventure. Jacob excitably says, "Gabby, give the next envelope."

The next envelope, Father intercepts and states, "I will open this one. I am used to the envelopes this size."

There is laughter throughout our living room. The envelope has instructions. Father proceeds to pull the folded paper out, and it is ten thousand dollars to spend on their trip.

Just as all the excitement was happening, Gabby's parents come through the kitchen. Gabby and Jacob gave Gabby's parents a trip and cash earlier. Gabby's parents and ours are traveling together on this little excursion. Mother says, "I am getting the food out on the serving table. We are celebrating Christmas Eve tonight!"

Everyone scurries throughout the house to get the gifts they got for each other. All will meet in the living room at the Christmas tree. Father helps mother after sending the boys to the barn to grab the two pieces of furniture he made for his girls' having his grandchildren. Father tells the boys, "Take the truck, you will need it!"

Father giggles a little, and the boys are wondering what they are bringing to the house. Joshua and Noah jump in the box of the truck. Jackson and Joe are in the front. Joe backs the truck into the barn, where Father's workshop is. Joshua turns the light on. Noah jumps out and starts to uncover the pieces of furniture. All the boys are looking at the beautiful work Father has done. Joe and Jackson agree, "The girls are going to love this!"

The guys back the truck to the porch on the living room side of the house to unload the gifts. The boys keep the pieces covered as they place the three pieces by the tree.

Mother calls everyone to eat. As we move to the dining room, Jacob and Jeremiah arrive. Everyone is home for Christmas Eve a night early. Our family eats, cleans the dishes off the table, and moves to the living room around the Christmas tree. Mother has the stereo playing old Christmas carols.

As she hands the girls the gifts from the boys, Father hands Mother her gift. Then Father gives Sarah and Rachel their gifts. They pull the furniture blankets off the gifts. Rachel says, "Father, this is beautiful!" Sarah cannot get over the workmanship of the three cradle swings.

Father says, "That should hold them while they sleep."

The girls say, "Thank you!"

Gabby's parents are admiring the cradles, chatting with Father how nice they are. The workmanship is impeccable.

Joe and Jeremiah carry the cradle swings by Joe and Sarah's room to make room for the family to get comfortable throughout the living room. The girls receive a nice piece of JEWELRY from their husbands. The girls, all adorned in their jewels, look at each other, complimenting the style and look of each piece.

The attention comes back to Jeremiah and Jacob. "We weren't expecting you home so soon," Father says excitedly.

Sophia says, "We are glad you are here!"

Ava adds, "What a nice surprise!"

Jeremiah asks Father, "Have you many new additions to the herd?"

"Oh my, yes! Are you kidding? Definitely. There are fourteen new editions," Noah states.

Joe comments, "We were in the barn for a few days and still have more mothers we are watching. It is soon time for at least five more to give birth."

Jackson adds, "Maybe it will happen while you are home. What an amazing event! When do you have to head back to Texas?"

Jackson, looking at Jacob, asks, "Arizona?"

Jeremiah looks at Sophia and says, "We will be leaving in a month."

Jacob states, "We leave right after New Year's Eve, the moving truck is coming to pick up all of our things from the cabin, and we must go," as he turns to look at Gabby, holding her hand and hugging her close.

Everyone can tell Gabby is excited but sad at the same time. Tears fill her eyes as she asks, "When is the moving truck coming?"

Jacob states, "The day after New Year's. I was hoping my brothers could come over and help move and pack things so everything is in the living room. This way the movers don't have to walk all through the house. We can take the beds apart, and Gabby can pack things into boxes and mark them with the room they will be in. When the movers get to our house, they will know what room to take them to. I figure we do not have to leave until a month or so."

Gabby asks, "What about when we get to the house in Arizona? I will need to unpack. Shouldn't we leave sooner?"

Jacob states, "Nah, your mother and father will let the movers in our house, put things where they need to be, and make sure the doors are locked."

Gabby now feels relieved but is wondering why her parents are on the other end of Arizona and so far from their home. "What are my parents doing near Phoenix?"

Jacob says, "Aren't you excited your parents are taking that job so we do not have to leave the ranch until a much later date?"

Gabby looks around the room. "Sure, but—"

"No, Gabs, we are done talking about moving. What are your thoughts with the Grilling Post? You can hire Sarah to run it for you and Rebekah to do the accounting part of the job so Sarah can run it to the best of her managing ability. You need to start thinking about what it is you will be doing with the restaurant."

Gabby states, "Sarah has good managing skills. Of course, that is what I will do. Sarah, you know what is going on and to have meetings with the staff once a month, twice if needed. The place basically runs itself. The staff is trusting. Maybe I should think about selling. I will wait and see what happens with Jacob and his job."

"Jeremiah, what about you?" Father asks. "What is the moving situation with you and Sophia?"

Sophia states, "I will do the same thing Gabby is doing. That sounds like a great idea to label the boxes."

Jeremiah states, "We only need to take boxes of personal items. Our furniture stays in the cabin. Our townhouse is 2,500 square feet of living space newly built, and the new furniture arrives two days before we get there. We are driving. I just figure I would pull a trailer from a rental facility and drop it at a sister rental facility in Texas. What are your thoughts, Sophia?"

"I can pack up our personal things. I doubt we will need a trailer. All I really need to take is our clothes and personal items. Please contact the movers and cancel since we won't need them to move anything for us. We will be fine with a suitcase in our Jeep."

Jeremiah reaches out to his residency liaison to notify them not to send a mover. "Hello, this is Jeremiah Sawyer. I am calling to decline the mover. Since we do not have to bring furniture, we will be moving what we need in our Jeep. Thank you for the offer. See you when we arrive. Yes, thank you. We will. Have a wonderful Christmas and Happy New Year as well." Jeremiah ends the call and goes back to the family.

Everyone moves to the dining room to help Mother set the food on the serving counter. My entire family stands around the table hand in hand while Father gives thanks for friends, family, food, health, the love of all, and how blessed we are to have each other in our lives. Amen.

We file through to the serving counter along the wall in the dining area. Father, Mother, and Gabby's parents are chatting about their trip and when they can arrange to take it. They sound ecstatically excited about leaving and being able to hang out together. Ava and Joshua are talking with Rachel and Jackson about the contractors, which ones they thought they would want to use and why.

There's a very deep discussion going on. Jeremiah and Sophia are discussing the drive and route they would like to take so they can take their time and see things along the way, trying to pinpoint a day to leave. Jeremiah is telling Sophia when he needs to be in Texas. Jeremiah also adds, "We need to leave early so we are not caught in the holiday traffic, or maybe we should look into taking the train. We can enjoy the trip a little better, and we can take our SUV on the train."

Jacob and Gabby are thinking maybe they will only take their bed set Father made and purchase other furniture for the rest of the house.

Noah and I are just hanging out, no worries at all. Rachel did mention a dress fitting Christmas Day or Christmas Eve. I am thinking Christmas Eve. I will ask her later. Noah tells me, "I am anxious about the new mothers in the barn, and I want to check on them."

I tell him, "I will walk out with you. It may be possible you need help. I'd like to get some fresh air as well."

Noah and I walk out to the barn and notice two of the mothers lying on the floor in labor. I quickly call into the house as I start to boil water. Father says he is on his way to the barn with Joe. Logan arrived at the barn to visit with Father and helps deliver the calves. I walk back into the house.

Mother is on the phone with Pastor Rob. The girls are in the living room, trying on their brides-maid dresses for my wedding. I walk in, and they are laughing, excited, and tell me the makeup artist, hair dresser, and dress fittings are tomorrow. I ask, "Tomorrow, December 24? Okay, I guess I will be ready for all that, especially since I can't wait to play through all this to see what I look like. Just make sure Noah does not see me!"

Sarah and Rachel look at each other, smile, and wink. The dresses look beautiful. The dresses are a shade of Christmas purple, with a smooth light-lav-ender shimmer throughout, a slit from floor to midthigh on the left side for a little peekaboo look when walking. The girls all agreed on a lavender flat slipper, comfy for all-night dancing or whatever the night might hold.

The flat screen turns on as Father flips through the channels to find a movie, probably a Western or action adventure. It's been four hours since the guys were out in the barn. They are sitting in the living room, and Father is talking about the cattle and the calves, the boys sitting with their wives—Rachel with her husband, Noah and with me, Logan with Bella. Mother finished in the kitchen and is on her way to the chair next to Father. Gabby's parents will be staying at the ranch until after the Christmas.

A SPECIAL CHRISTMAS

I head to the bathroom to shower and pass Noah on the way. I reach for my toothbrush. He tells me to text him when breakfast is ready. He is heading out to the barn with my brothers to do the chores. I tell him sure thing as I close the door to the bathroom and spit toothpaste from my mouth in the sink. I shower and wrap my hair in the towel; it is going to be a no makeup day today.

The house phone is ringing off the hook. Mother answers one call after another. I try to answer the phone when I get to the kitchen, only to have her look to me with her don't-even eyes and sends me in another direction. I walk in through the dining area to the living room and notice the round tables are being placed throughout the dining area and into the kitchen. Our farmhouse table is now along the kitchen wall under the window by the kitchen door.

Mother talks in short sentences while she makes breakfast. She places the food on the serving counter then calls everyone to eat. I text Noah to let him know breakfast is ready, but he is already walking in the door with my brothers, loudly laughing. Bella is helping Mother in the kitchen. They are talking like a bunch of chickens in a henhouse. I think those two are up to something, laughing, whispering, then a giggle here and there. They will say something out loud and go back to huddled whispering. Hmm, I just wonder what they could be up to.

Father is in the living room in his chair with a coffee and his newspaper. I stroll in and sit with my father to see why Mother has all the round tables with the fresh linen throughout the kitchen and dining area. Father says, "I believe there is some sort of party or gathering this evening. I'm not really sure."

He lifts the paper back up to see the article he was reading. "You know, Rebekah, I do remember Mother calling the families whose children do not have off work to come home for Christmas, so we have reached out and invited many friends this Christmas to the ranch."

I say, "Oh, I wonder if there is anything I can do. I was not aware of all this, although I do think I remember Mother saying about the families coming, but I did not know it was a done deal."

Father replied, "I think this was last minute. If your mother needs your help, she will ask. She does have Bella's help, and they look like they have it under control."

Father is flipping through the channels. He finds Christmas movies, and I curl up on the recliner next to him. In no time at all, I am sleeping. Hours go by.

Mother tells Noah, "The Tall Pines Tuxedo Shop delivered everyone's tux and accessories and they are in Joe and Sarah's room. Can you take them to the third floor please?"

Noah hugs mother. "Thank you. I don't think she suspects a thing! I will notify the guys. This may be an easy surprise this evening." Noah smiles and makes his way upstairs to the third floor.

Lit candles are placed on the tables. Sophia brings flowered swags, centerpieces, and boutonnieres in from Mother's room. Sarah takes the boutonnieres to the third floor for the guys, and the bouquets stay in Mother and Father's room for the girls. Father remains in his chair so as to not wake me. Rachel gets a text from her photographer. The plane has landed. She will be at the ranch in twenty minutes.

Sarah pushes the girls into Mother's room to get hair and makeup done. Sarah tells them, "We want to be dressed before Rebekah wakes."

They all agree and rush to Mother and Father's room with Mother and Bella right behind them. Father has to get up in a bit to get dressed, and this move might wake me. He figures he will wait as long as he can. Pastor Rob has arrived. He sits with Father, talking softly. The Grilling Post staff arrive. They take over the kitchen. They take the meat out of the heat boxes and place them to cook the rest of the time needed in the wall ovens as the sauces and sides are made. Now the kitchen is busy.

I stir a little, sit up, move a little, and am now lying with my back against Father. Father felt me moving and then decided to scoot out of the chair and place a pillow along my back. Father swiftly walks to the third floor with the guys. Pastor Rob giggles at what just took place. Allianna brought Pastor Rob a coffee. Ashton and Avery arrive, and they have direction from my brother Joe where to park the cars.

Sarah wakes me after another hour passes. She takes me by the hand so I don't look around the room too much to notice the transformation that took place while I was sleeping. I am rubbing at my eyes, trying to get my bearings as I am led into my parents' room. I wipe my eyes one last time and see my dress hanging by the window in my mother's room. I start to walk toward the dress, but I feel a tug and a light push to a chair. Lyndra, our hair stylist, removes the towel from my head and the makeup artist from the photo shoots in New York is putting my face on. My hair smells good. As a matter of fact, it is still really wet from the shower I took earlier this morning.

Before I know it, my makeup is done, my hair looks freaking gorgeous, and when I get up from the chair, I step into my dress so I can see what I look like when my big day arrives. My sister Rachel is fastening me into the elegant dress. I am busy helping her hold ends, and then she places the veil on my head, and it is fastened to the updo with stringy ringlets. Just then, the door to Mother's bedroom opens, and it's Ethan from New York. She is going to take a couple of snapshots of the pre-dress gathering. While the camera is flashing, I turn to look at myself in the mirror. As I look in the mirror, I notice my sisters standing behind me. They are smiling. Their hair and makeup are perfect, and I tell them, "This is exactly what I want us all to look like on my wedding day!" They are all looking at me with giggles and smiles as the door opens to the bedroom, and my father enters the room in his tux. I hear music. It is the Rat Pack singing Christmas songs softly from Mother's stereo downstairs.

Mother comes from the master bathroom. She looks amazing. The door to the bedroom opens once more, and now I hear people. The house is full of people. Pastor Rob knocks, gets the okay from Sarah to open the door, sticks his head in, and says, "Don't you all look beautiful. Are we ready?"

I look around the room and say, "Ready? What? Oh my! Am I getting married now? This Christmas Eve! How did all this happen? I look at Rachel, and she reminds me, "We went over everything a million times, I think we got this!"

Father says, "I think it is time to head out to see everyone, to gather with Noah and the rest of your family. Noah planned the wedding for late afternoon. Are you ready to see the groom?"

Father smiles, takes me by the arm, and says, "Wait for it." Father reaches for the lever of the bedroom door. He looks at me and tells me how beautiful I look. He opens the door. The living room has a handful of chairs with close friends and family waiting for the last of the Sawyer siblings to get married.

My wedding dress is made of taffeta, shimmer champagne color, sweetheart corset bodice, swept length with a cathedral train. My hair is bunched up kind of messy with stray ringlet curls, and my makeup is flawless. Everyone has their eyes on me.

We make our way through the guests and find ourselves coming to Noah, my brothers, and my sisters. The photographer snaps pictures as we leave the bedroom behind us and make our way through the candlelight to Noah and the rest of my family waiting with Pastor Rob by the Christmas tree on the other side of the living room. Noah has a smile as big as Texas with tears rolling down his face as he mouths, "You look like an angel."

Pastor Rob asks my father, "Who gives Rebekah, the bride, to her groom?"

My father reaches for my mother. They smile as they look at each other to say, "We do." They look to Pastor Rob as he joins Noah and my hands together. Father and Mother take a seat in the two front chairs.

I am so excited inside. I just want to jump and holler. Noah and I follow Pastor Rob to our Christmas tree. The flash from the photographer goes on through the entire ceremony. Pastor Rob begins to speak, telling everyone how Noah came to him soon after he arrived in town to chat about a wedding. Pastor Rob stated, "I have never seen such an overanxious young man to marry a young lady before in all my days of counseling. We spoke for hours about

Rebekah. I had no question Rebekah was going to be the luckiest young lady in the world. This young boy was not a boy with frivolous, contrary thinking, but instead, this boy was not a boy at all. He is in fact a young man with plans and thoughts of life to share with his bride, Rebekah. These two are definitely going to have a love that lasts forever."

Pastor Rob turns to Rebekah. He says, "You are a stunning bride. I am assuring you Noah is ready to be your husband, and he loves you very much. I am telling you things you should already know"—the guests giggle a little. "These two have written their vows to each other. Rebekah, Noah."

I start, "I know there are going to be days we want to throw in the towel."

Noah replies, "Never. We will ride the storms no matter how treacherous and angry."

I say, "I love you, and every day with you feels like the first day we met. I still tingle inside when you look at me. I get butterflies in my stomach when you touch and hold me. I don't want to ever argue or fight with you. There will be no disagreements, only compromise."

Noah says, "I feel your butterflies. I feel your tingles. I hear it in your voice, even when you sleep. I love you till the day I die. There will be no one else before you, and there are no differences, no arguing, fighting, or disagreeing. We are two that will always be one. I know you are the boss."

Our guests burst out laughing. Noah looks at the guests and adds, "I know what I'm saying. You all had to learn the women are the boss in your household. I know. I'm not stupid."

He smiles and looks to me. The guests are still laughing at Noah's statement; they are trying to hold it together until the end of the ceremony.

That being said, my brother Joe hands Noah a tiny band. Noah reaches across, holds my left hand, and as he places a white-gold wedding band of channel diamonds on my finger, Noah states, "I love you today, tomorrow, and always. This ring's diamonds are brighter because you make them sparkle, and it is a symbol of my love for you that is never-ending." Noah lifts my hand; he kisses it softly.

My sister Rachel hands me the same type of ring but larger and wider. I profess my love for Noah as never-ending and place the ring on his finger.

Noah pulls me close and holds me tight as we kiss. The guests are whistling, clapping, and yelling that Rebekah, the last of the Sawyers, is married. Pastor Rob congratulates us as we turn to the guests, and Pastor Rob pronounces us Mr. and Mrs. Noah Ramsey.

We work our way through our family and friends to the table reserved for us and our wedding party. The Christmas song "(There's No Place Like) Home for the Holidays" comes on, and Noah pulls me to the front of the Christmas tree to dance. Noah tells me, "This is our wedding song. I know how much you love Christmas. I know being with family is a large part of your life. You would never leave this place. I understand why. Your family is amazing. All your brothers and sister—this is who you are. This is where I want to be the rest of my life…with you."

He holds me close. Guests are tapping on their glasses for us to kiss. We kiss, and he dips me. The photographer's flash goes off again. The song ends, and we return to our table with our family while guests are clapping.

The wait staff from the Grilling Post are busy working the room. My table and immediate family are served. After dinner, Noah and I make our way around the room to welcome our guests, thanking them for coming, chatting, and catching up with some we don't get to see much. We finally end with my parents, siblings, and Gabby's parents, Bella and Logan.

The photographer has taken many candid shots, highlights of the ceremony, and the dinner. Ethan is asking the family to gather together so pictures can be taken by the fireplace, Christmas tree, the staircase, and the barn with Duchess. She also suggests taking pictures outside with the full moon glistening off the snow and that we should do the outside pictures first.

The Christmas music plays all night. Our guests were given cupcakes and assorted pastries, soda, coffee, tea, or milk after dinner. Four hours have gone by. Our guests are heading out as the wait staff and kitchen staff are cleaning up the tables and kitchen. Avery and Ashton are bringing the guests' cars to the front of the house. My brothers and Jackson are breaking down the tables. They are placing them on the veranda along with the folding chairs for the pavilion staff from the Grilling Post to pick up in the morning.

Ethan, Noah, and I are back from the barn. Ethan is asking if the family is ready for the photos with Noah and me. Pictures go on for another two hours. The photographer has been here since 3:00 p.m., around the time everyone was getting ready for the wedding. The time is now 11:30 p.m.; it's been a long day. I am exhausted. Noah is tired as well. Ethan tells me once the photos are processed, she would like me to review and okay the ones of my getting-ready-for-the-ceremony photos while I was getting dressed.

I say, "Sure, we can look at them to okay them for you, and was just wondering, will you be sending them to Rachel's e-mail?"

Ethan says, "Yes, I will be sending them to Rachel. I want to make sure you are okay with the ones I will be placing in the magazine and on Rachel's Internet page."

Ethan hugs Rachel, and she is on her way to the Wolf's Den Hotel.

Everyone has gone home. The Christmas songs are still playing softly on Mother's stereo. Pictures are complete. Father comes from the bedroom, stating he does not mind dressing up, but he sure is glad to be in his PJs. Mother states she is taking a shower to get the hair spray out of her hair and then coming back out to sit with Father on his comfy chair. My siblings and their spouses are exhausted. They are talking among themselves and patting themselves on the back for being able to pull this off. I look at them and say, "This was the strangest wedding I have ever been to, strange because the bride is to be prepared, not *surprised*, for her wedding! I loved it! This moment will be remembered all my life as the biggest surprise ever!"

Noah states, "I had your sisters put today's date on the invitations and send them out immediately.

I wanted to marry you this Christmas. I could not wait! We just told you May so you would be relaxed and not so stressed since I had so much help. I would like to thank my favorite brothers and sisters for helping me pull this one off!"

As my brothers, Jackson and Noah, head upstairs, they agree with Father the tux has to go! They assure Mother their tux will be hung on the hangers so they may be returned as soon as the shop opens, and they will be downstairs for a cupcake and ice cream since they were busy cleaning up. Mother stated, "Someone could use our master bath." Jacob and Gabby run to Mother and Father's room.

The rooms that once held guests are all back in order. The decorations for our wedding are all packed up and ready for storage at the Grilling Post.

The guys come to the living room. Father talks to the boys about how easy it was to pull the wedding off and not cause any craziness for me. The guys are scattered throughout the living room, yelling for us girls to get a shower and join them, only to fall asleep in the living room for the night.

NEW YEAR'S EVE

I ask Rachel, Gabby, Ava, and Sophia what we can plan for New Year's Eve. Joe and Sarah were married New Year's Eve. They were married under the large oak tree in the yard at 11:20 p.m. That oak tree looked sensational. We decorated it with white LED Christmas lights and lit the path from the house to the tree with candles in white luminary bags.

Sarah wore a beautiful dress with a white fur-lined hooded cloak and hand muff of fur that matched. Joe was dressed in jeans with a black jacket, white dress shirt, and a maroon tie with his cowboy boots. We had guests, but only a few stood under the oak tree to watch the ceremony while others sat on our porch, facing the tree. Jim from the feed mill borrowed a few outdoor heaters from his feed store rental department that helped keep the guests warm

on the porch while Pastor Rob performed the ceremony under the tree.

"So what are your thoughts?" I asked.

Gabby started by saying, "I already have the
food ordered. Ribs, pulled pork, and baked beans
with rolls, pickles, and other finger foods. I had the
Grilling Post staff prepare the food before they were
done for the holiday. All we have to do is heat the
food and place it on the dining serving counter for
New Year's Eve."

Sarah replies, "We just want to celebrate and
be with family before everyone leaves. Who knows
when we will see, or I should say, be together again
for a holiday."

Ava says, "I will make my grandmother's barbe-
cue with steamed rolls."

Sarah, Rachel, and Sophia are talking among
themselves to make a dish to go with what is coming from the Grilling Post. They are possibly making
fries with toppings.

Father will have rocking Times Squares New
York's Eve on the flat screen with all the popular
singers to bring in the New Year. He likes to flip to
see the New Year come in around the world, so we
are up for a while after we hit midnight and toast

to the New Year. Noah says, "Abigail's kitchen never sleeps." Abigail smiles.

Mother roasted a thirty-pound turkey glazed with her family-secret honey glaze. The turkey breasts are always juicy. Gabby and Sophia cooked their famous seafood chowder with crab, lobster, shrimp, baby clams, a few cut-up potatoes, onions, and a lot of other goodies. Ava made large mushrooms stuffed with lump crabmeat, sprinkled with white imported cheddar cheese.

Sarah made the seven large beef tenderloin after taking a few of our steers to the butcher this past fall. Sarah had them cut into one-and-three-quarter-inch slices. They were placed in her secret bourbon marinade for two weeks, flipping, shaking, and adding more marinade when needed. These steaks will melt in your mouth come time to eat New Year's when they are coming off the grill. I am getting so hungry for tomorrow night; my stomach is growling. Sarah will make her twice-baked potatoes, stuffed with potato, of course, and shredded shards of veggies topped with a sprinkle of Monterey Jack cheese. We bake cookies as we always do the night before a holiday to add a little sparkle to the food table.

We set up the dining room table and placed the linen tablecloth with a few sticks of sparkle to be festive this holiday. Noah states, "Life just does not slow down around here. Your family starts out with Thanksgiving dinner, and their dinner parties continue throughout New Year's Eve."

I notify Noah, "Yes, but then after New Year's Eve, it is all over. This year will be much different. After the first of the year, Jeremiah will be off to his residency with Sophia, and Jacob will be going to Arizona with Gabby. Things will calm down after the holidays. It seems everything is always busy from Thanksgiving until New Year's."

It is New Year's Eve. Father has a nice crackling fire in the fireplace, and the food is being prepped for the evening of a wonderful dinner. The boys placed champagne on ice with Mother's glasses arranged at the end of the buffet table in the dining room. Father moved to the kitchen to carve the turkey and places it back in its juice. He placed the turkey on the warmer in the large stainless steel roaster. Ava has all the veggies ready and in their warmers. The steaks will be made to order off the grill on the back porch. I ask Joe for a medium-rare steak. He grabs the bag of steaks from the cooler and heads to the veranda to get the grill started with his brothers and a handful of friends. Joe tells Ava, Sophia, and Rachel to take orders as to how the guys want their steaks grilled.

The guys are gathered around the grill to keep the chill off, talking about Joe's being a dad and how his life is going to change. A little person watching everything from his actions to his words. I return to Joe with the list of how we want our steaks done.

Everyone brings their champagne glass to eye level. Father starts the toast of the last holiday before the boys leave for their work assignments. "May everyone's New Year be prosperous. May our new editions be healthy, and we know they will bring joy to our family." The glasses are held high. Everyone nods and presses the glass to their lips for a sip.

The girls are all sitting around Sarah, talking about her, the responsibilities of the Grilling Post, and the patter of little feet running the house and making decisions for her. Mother is at the food table, scooping the glaze over the turkey slices, stirring the veggies, and checking on the chowder. Sarah, Ava, and Sophia pull the fries out of the oven and top them with baked beans, cheddar, and pulled pork. Gabby says, "These are delicious. We should sell these at the bar as a snack for customers to order. We can call them Grilling Post fries. I will run that by Chef Shay to see what her thoughts are on the new bar pickin' food."

We all fill our plates and sit to watch the dropping of the ball in Times Square on the flat screen.

MOVING ON...

*J*eremiah and Sophia left two weeks ago for their train ride to Texas. They packed their clothes, and off they went. They notified the family of their arrival in Texas four days after they left the ranch. They told us the train is the way to go. Sophia talked about the private sleeping rooms, dining car, café/lounge car and stated they relaxed, ate wonderful food, met a lot of interesting people, and enjoyed the time they spent together on the trip south, plus they loaded their SUV, which was a great convenience.

As for Gabby and Jacob, the movers stopped by their cabin January 2 to pick up furniture and their boxed items should arrive in Arizona in two days. Gabby's parents have kept in contact with the movers as they traveled so they could meet them when they arrive. Gabby's phone rings, and it is her mother calling to ask for their new home address. She is telling Gabby she is in the development and just needs the house number and the name of the road. I hear Gabby say, "The address is 1225 Coyote Avenue. Jacob said it is a large corner lot. Let me check my text message from him and I will tell you. Yes, it is Coyote Avenue and Armadillo Way. Did the movers arrive? Is everything okay?"

Her mother then says, "Oh my…"

Gabby's facial expression changes to one of concern as she asks, "Is there something wrong? Jacob was told the house is completed. Are you at the correct address?"

Gabby listens as her parents are now on speaker phone. "Gabby," her mother says, "the house is completed. It is the largest one in the entire development. Hold on, we are making our way through the gate onto the property. Your landscaping is amazing. The entrance to your home is very welcoming, and you have an in-ground pool, pool house, and grilling entertaining area. My gosh! Gabby, what exactly does Jacob do again?"

There is relief in Gabby's tone when she replies, "Jacob is a nuclear physicist, Mother. I thought you and I spoke about this. I know Jacob told Father."

Gabby's mother, Bella, asks, "Have you seen the house completed or a blueprint of the house before it was started?"

Gabby states, "Well, Jacob teamed up with Joshua and Ava on a few sketches, then they forwarded his ideas to an architect in Arizona who attended college with them. Why, Mother, Father? Is there something alarming I should know about?"

"No. Everything is fine, Gabby."

Logan, Gabby's father, tells Bella, "Time to hang up, Bell, the movers are at the gate. We need to let them in so we can tell them where to place Gabby and Jacob's things."

Gabby's mother says her goodbyes and tells Gabby they will stay at the house to work on putting their things where they belong. Gabby thanks her and ends the call, "Goodbye. Don't do all my work. Thank you so much! Love you both!"

Gabby hangs up and is very anxious to get to Arizona. Gabby says, "If the house is that large, I will have my parents stay with us. Their room should be on the first floor. I know we have a master suite on the first and second floors. I should tell my parents to have the movers place our bedroom furniture and clothes in the master on the second floor."

Gabby calls her parents to tell them about placing Jacob and her bedroom furniture in the second floor master suite. Her parents thank her for calling to notify them of the change. The call ends quickly so they can inform the movers, and they can carry the furniture to the appropriate room on the second floor.

Now that Gabby and Jacob are moving, their cabin may be a home rented by a ranch hand. I am sure Joe thought of that already. I will mention it when we eat dinner tonight.

Jacob and Gabby spend the last day with the family on the ranch before leaving for Arizona to their home in the rural area of Desert View Estates. We all wished them safe travels as they say their goodbyes and go on their way. Father and Mother promised to visit after they get back from their trip with Gabby's parents in three months. We all walked to the porch to watch as their SUV drove out the driveway.

Father turns to Mother, and tears are in her eyes. "Don't cry. We spoke about this day when those three would possibly be leaving the ranch after college. This is a wonderful time for Jacob and Gabby. They get to spread their wings."

Mother nods her head yes as Father hugs her and tells her, "We still have Joshua, Joe, Rachel, and Rebekah with their spouses. We have Rachel and Jackson back, and the holidays will only be better when Jacob and Gabby fly in." Mother says, "I am okay. I did know this day was coming. It just seems like yesterday I was changing diapers, homeschooling, then high school and college days, and now we are at the point where they leave the ranch. I am going to miss those four."

Mother turns and goes into the house, and Father follows her.

Happenings

It is five months into the new year. Rachel's baby, Sebastian Jackson, is due July 4. The summer house has been renovated and remodeled to Rachel and Jackson's liking. They used three contractors of the seven and the house was completed in no time. They are in their office from the time they get up until late every night. Jackson's plan is to work days in advance so he can take some time off when Rachel has the baby.

Jackson dabbles a little in the Wall Street business, working stocks for clients, and is working for a few local businesses, doing their accounting, payroll, balancing books, and submitting payment on bills to run the business. He is one part of a checks-and-balances protocol set in the many local businesses he works for in our town and surrounding towns. Jackson will manage his time so he may spend more time with Rachel and their baby when Sebastian arrives. Jackson and Rachel's work ethic is dedicated to working to complete clients' demands.

Joe and Sarah's daughter, Abigail Grace, was born May 22. She is such a little cutie. Sarah was to have identical twins, but there were complications with Palmer, and she passed after she was born. Palmer was cremated and will be laid to rest with my brother or sister-in-law when they pass. For now, she is on the mantel of the fireplace in the living room of the ranch house.

Father places a flower in a small vase by Palmer's urn every day. It was a sad time at our ranch, a tragic, horrible time for my family, for everyone. Father tells us Palmer is a guardian angel for a child who needed her more than we did. Palmer is doing bigger and better things. We will see her beautiful glowing face when we get to heaven. Father always knows what to say to comfort his family.

This tragic loss prompted counseling from Pastor Rob. He is trying to have us embrace death as we do life, love, and happiness. We enjoy Pastor Rob's visits. Understanding death is just as complicated as understanding life. Pastor Rob doesn't give up on his church or his congregation. He has helped our family more than once. This won't be the last. Pastor Rob helps us look at things in a different light, so to speak.

Jeremiah and Sophia are doing well. They are expecting their first child March of next year. They are excited to know the sex of the baby in a few weeks. Sophia talks with Mother every night and tells her she is extremely sick all day, not just in the morning. Mother keeps telling her it does not happen only in the morning, it can happen all day, anytime of the day. According to Sophia, Jeremiah is doing great in his fellowship. Sophia is really homesick. She cannot wait until the five years of residency are completed for Jeremiah. Mother said, "You can set your clock by Sophia's phone calls. The calls are every night, 8:00 p.m.—sharp no sooner, no later."

We spoke to Jacob and Gabby a few weeks ago. Jacob was working on a top secret project for the government even though this is something Gabby did not want him to do. Gabby said the pay is really good. She is hopeful that one day soon, they can share the news of a little one on the way. Unlike Sarah and Rachel, they were tossing around baby names. Fiona Madison if it's a girl, and Xander Ryker if it's a boy. Gabby and Jacob are excited that one day soon, children will come into the picture. I miss everyone already!

Father and Mother are in the dining room, trying to get their photos into albums so we can see what they did and where they went on their trip. The dining room looks like the camera exploded. Father says the photos are laid out on the dining room table in some organized way.

I am doing some business on the computer at the desk in the living room. I hear my parents laughing and reminiscing about their trip with Gabby's parents. They sound like a young married couple home from their honeymoon. I can only hope Noah and I are as happy when we reach their age.

Noah and I have been so busy in different directions lately. We see each other for breakfast, lunch, and dinner, then there are the Pastor Rob sessions of family counseling and sleep. I need to see if we can get some ride time scheduled in so we can at least catch up with each other. I get a hug or a smooch in passing. Time and life go fast. Maybe some time after the cattle are out in the grazing area we will be able to get away for a while, maybe a week or just a weekend to hang out and catch up.

I make my way to the sofa, tired from crunching numbers for the ranch. I lay with my feet up on the back of the sofa, head on the armrest. My thoughts are focused on all I have to do to make things balanced, which in turn will prompt Sarah to schedule a cattle pickup in a few weeks. I wonder if we could have two pickup times as we have more than enough young cattle raised.

Although Father wants to hold on to some little ones, I will have to call a meeting with Sarah, Joe, Father, and Noah to see what is best for the ranch. I will place a meeting in one of the calendar days we are not busy next week. I go back to the computer and try to figure out how to schedule a meeting. Let me see how this works. She showed me once; it did not look that hard to do.

> 10 am Meeting in the living room for your thoughts on two cattle pickups before the cattle go to graze.

Perfect! Now I wait to see if I get four check marks on this scheduled meeting, then it is final. I will check back later on the meeting acceptance. I am glad our holidays are not like this. Jeez, our family is so busy, they would never get together.

Mother is inviting me to sit on the swing at the east corner of the veranda. She is enticing me with a bowl of ice cream. I check to make sure the scheduled meeting is set in stone and see there are three check marks out of four. Noah did not check yet. Okay, so I did it correctly. I am on my way to the porch to Mother, and the house phone rings.

UNCERTAIN NEWS

*F*ather answers the phone. I hear concern in his tone. He does not know what to say. Mother makes her way back in the house. She is hovering, trying to catch some of the conversation but cannot pick out what is being said. She waits patiently as she watches my father. Father is nodding his head. "What you are telling me is that…they are missing? Where were they last seen? Should we come to help search? Okay, sure. We have not heard from them in a while. I am thinking a month if not more? We thought they were busy with the house, settling in to the new job. Okay, thank you for calling."

Father, with his head down, looks to me then Mother. He then asks, "Where are the boys? We need to make a call to Jeremiah and Sophia so they do not hear anything from the news. I don't even know what I am saying to them right now. I am not sure. Please call them, Abigail. I need to speak with them."

Mother states, "The boys are in the barn with the cattle, getting ready to move them to the grazing area. Why?" She is dialing Sophia's number as father requested.

Father states, "Rebekah, please run out to the barn and collect everyone. Bring them to the house."

I reach the barn and get everyone's attention, "Hey, guys, you need to get to the house now. Father has something to tell everyone."

I quickly run back to the house and sit on the sofa with Rachel, Sarah, Ava, and Mother. We all await the news anxiously from Father. Mother could not reach Jeremiah and Sophia on Sophia's cell number, so Father tells Sarah to get Sophia on the smart screen.

In a few moments, Sarah has Sophia and Jeremiah on the smart screen virtually. All the boys are in from the barn. Father tells everyone what was just told to him on the phone. Father states, "I received a call from Colorado State Police. All I know is Gabby and Jacob are presumed missing. I am not sure how, why, or what exactly happened. I am not sure. I am not sure what to think until I know the facts. I just wanted all of you hearing it from me first. I was not sure if this would be broadcast over national news.

"The person on the phone told me that Jacob and Gabby did not survive. They also mentioned missing, so there is a *big* difference between the two. There is a gentleman supposed to stop by the ranch and speak to us. Gabby's parents will be arriving later as well. As soon as we know what happened, we will contact all of you. We are going to say they are missing until they find bodies, God forbid." We all give our farewells. "Be careful and stay safe. Talk to you more when we know more." Father tells everyone to keep Gabby and Jacob in their prayers. Everyone is deeply concerned and worried about Gabby and Jacob.

The screen goes black. Jeremiah called Father on his cell to talk to him more." I hear Father say, "Hello, Jeremiah. We are not sure of anything. No, can't tell you that for sure. Don't worry. He is smart. Not sure what to say. Let's just wait to see what the gentleman that is to arrive today says, then we may be able to put the pieces together and figure out what happened. Yes, Jeremiah, will do. You and Sophia take care of yourselves and don't believe anything you hear on the national news if this story hits. Wait to hear from me. Goodbye. Love you both too."

The phone call ends, and there is a knock at the door.

ABOUT THE AUTHOR

Robin Miller lives within the central part of Pennsylvania in the mountains with her husband, who is extremely supportive of Robin. This story and series of books holds some events of Robin's life. Her great-grandparents had a dairy farm, and her grandfather was a well-known blacksmith, not to mention an avid horse rider. Robin and her grandfather spent a lot of time riding horses together on the mountain trails where she lives. Her family had a simple life. Nothing about Robin's family was rich or elaborate, although what they had was special to her.

This story is fictional. Only a few actual events, which are faint in the story like a breath of air, may be revealed by readers who personally know Robin. Enjoy the *Shimmering Meadow Ranch* series as she enjoys writing them.

CPSIA information can be obtained
at www.ICGtesting.com
Printed in the USA
LVHW040102020423
743250LV00005B/48

9 781638 819950